FLORA
LA FRESCA

& THE ART OF FRIENDSHIP

FLORA
LA FRESCA
& THE ART OF FRIENDSHIP

Veronica Chambers

illustrated by Sujean Rim

Dial Books for Young Readers

DIAL BOOKS FOR YOUNG READERS
An imprint of Penguin Random House LLC, New York

First published in the United States of America by Dial Books for Young Readers,
an imprint of Penguin Random House LLC, 2023

Text copyright © 2023 by Veronica Chambers
Illustrations copyright © 2023 by Sujean Rim

Visit us online at PenguinRandomHouse.com.

Library of Congress Cataloging-in-Publication Data is available.

Printed in the United States of America
ISBN 9780525556299

1st Printing
LSCH

Design by Cerise Steel
Text set in Eureka Pro

For the real Flora and Clara

¡Queridas!

Your easy, funny, friendship inspired this book.—V.C.

To everlasting friendships—S.R.

CHAPTER 1

Chica, Chica, Chica

Flora Violeta Lefevre despised a great many things, but few of them as much as Saturday Spanish school. They called it a school, but it was really just a classroom at the Westerly Education Center. The class was roughly a dozen students, all between the ages of seven and twelve. Like Flora, they all had Latine parents who wanted their kids to speak better Spanish but were too busy to teach them at home.

Their teacher was an indefatigable young woman named Señorita María José who was so energetic that Flora suspected that her gold hoop earrings and jangly bracelets were actually solar panels. They were allowed to call her by her first name because it was Saturday school. They were not allowed to ask her why she had a girl's name and a boy's name.

"It's just one of those things," she had said.

Señorita María José, or Srta. MJ for short, had grown up in Puerto Rico and was now getting her master's in teaching at Brown University.

All of the parents in Westerly, the town where Flora lived, said *Brown University* in a hushed and reverent tone, the same way the priest said *our Lord and Savior* during Sunday service. Flora's mother said, "We are so lucky to have María José teaching you Spanish. That woman is brilliant!"

Flora didn't have anything against her teacher. What she did have a problem with was spending practically half of one of her two days off doing extra school just because her parents were from Panama. But her parents made her go from nine a.m. to twelve noon, every Saturday no matter what excuse she could invent, from the time her eyesight "disappeared" to the violent stomachache that was really excellent acting for a ten-year-old, as anybody would tell you.

It would have been the worst except for the girl sitting next to her, who was the very best. Flora, who was ten and in the fifth grade, looked over at her best friend, Clara. Clarita slowly and deliberately rolled both of her eyes to the center of her head.

Flora tried, and failed, to stifle a giggle.

The lesson that day was about reflexive verbs, which made no sense to Flora. *Cállate la boca* was the only reflexive phrase Flora could say with confidence. But if she ever told her big sister to shut her mouth, she would get into more trouble than she knew what to do with.

"A verb is reflexive when the subject and the receiver are the same," Señorita MJ told the class. "For example, I washed the plate, not reflexive. I took a shower, reflexive."

Flora laid her head on the table. It didn't make sense. None of it made sense.

She was hoping to settle in for a teeny-tiny nap when she felt a note come sliding across the table.

Flora opened it up and grinned. It said:

Perk up, buttercup.

Flora looked over at Clara, who pretended to nap on the table, snored loudly, then pantomimed waking up and looking around as if she were completely disoriented.

Flora's Spanish was far from perfect, but she knew

that Clara was muy graciosa. Perhaps even the very funniest of all BFFs.

When the clock struck noon, Srta. María José said, "Okay chicos, you are free to go. Disfruten de su sábado."

Flora grabbed her navy-blue peacoat and dashed for the door. "¡Hasta whenever, Señorita María José!" she called out as she exited the classroom.

"Wait for me, Flora la Fresca!" Clara bellowed.

It was Clara's nickname for Flora and it had started the previous summer when Clara had taken the windbreaker that she wore around her waist and tied it around her shoulders. Then she took out a golden paper crown from the back pocket of her denim shorts and put it on Flora's head. She said, "I, Queen Clara, now residing in the realm of Westerly, have found you, Flora, to be the embodiment of all that is fun and good. From this day on, you shall be known as Flora la Fresca."

Sometimes the kids at school called her Flo, which Flora hated. But she liked Flora la Fresca. Even her parents called her that sometimes. If she wasn't exactly fresca—meaning fresh with a little bit of attitude—she definitely aspired to be.

Flora thought of that day as she waited for her friend.

Clara threw her quilted silver vest over her bright yellow sweatshirt and did a TikTok dance out of the room.

Flora said, "Come on, Clara!" but she didn't really mind waiting for her to start walking home. Everything was more fun when Clara was around. It was mid-November, but the day was warm like September as the girls walked through Wilcox Park and headed toward the ocean.

Westerly was a pretty little town on the coast of Rhode Island. Two and a half hours from New York and ninety minutes from Boston, it was a popular summer getaway. Most of the year, there were fewer than twenty thousand people in the town. It sounded like a lot, but it wasn't really. There were only thirty kids in the fifth grade of their public school, and Flora and Clara knew them all, as well as their siblings and parents. Once Memorial Day rolled around, the town's population doubled. The girls noticed that the streets filled with the faces of strangers as the big summer houses on the ocean's edge, which sat empty most of the winter, swelled with wealthy families and their guests.

Flora's uncle Rogelio, her mother's oldest brother, had moved to the town thirty years before to work at the quarry. Westerly Quarry was famous for its natural pink stone. Tío Rogelio had done well there and as he rose in the company, he got jobs for more and more Panamanians. Soon there were more than two dozen Panamanian families living in the small New England town.

Her uncle said that Westerly reminded him of Panama—not the cold or the snow, but how on a warm summer day, you could wake up and smell the briny saltiness of the Atlantic Ocean. Even if you couldn't see it, you could smell it. Tío said, "Where the sea is, we're home."

Flora stood in the middle of the park and took a big sniff.

Clara looked over at her and raised one eyebrow, then the other.

"Oh Flora," her friend said. "Are you smelling the sea again?"

Flora nodded.

Clara said, "Then I'll just have to take you there in my boat."

She pretended to drag an invisible canoe across the park gravel, then stopped midway and mimed dropping the end of the canoe. "Flora! It's heavy. Aren't you going to help?"

Flora went to where she imagined the back of the boat to be. She pushed at the air and Clara pulled.

Clara looked up and said, "Come on, Flora. Being invisible doesn't make the boat any lighter. Put some muscle into it."

Flora smiled and took a step back and pushed as if her life depended on it.

Clara looked up approvingly and said, "Chica, that's how it's done."

She stepped oh-so-carefully into the invisible canoe and gestured for Flora to join her.

Flora stepped in and sat cross-legged behind her friend.

Without needing to say a word, the girls began to move their invisible oars in unison. Sure they knew they looked goofy, but they were busy creating their own world.

"A la derecha," Clara whispered softly. "A la izquierda."

They sat that way, legs crisscrossed, moving their hands in semi-circles as if their fingers were oars and the gravel was the deepest blue ocean.

Flora said, "My dad said that when I'm sixteen, I can take sailing lessons."

Every summer Sunday, early before her mother and sister woke up, Flora and her father would walk to the Westerly boat yard and look at the boats heading out for the day. Her father, Santiago LeFevre, was tall, with a scraggly beard and a smile that was never far from his face. He would drink coffee, she would drink a babyccino—steamed milk with cocoa powder—and they would talk about boats. Flora dreamed about being able to sail a boat, the way her sister talked about getting a driver's license.

Clara kept paddling. "Great, I'll take sailing lessons when I'm sixteen too."

People passed them in the park, but no one seemed to notice their invisible canoe.

"Do you remember that girl Liba Daniels who used

to pick us up from school when we were in the third grade?"

Flora said "third grade" as if it had been *eons* ago and not just two years before.

Clara nodded and said, "Claro, Liba was cool."

Flora said, "My dad told me that Liba got her sailing license and she's taking a gap year from college. She's sailing some rich person's boat from Rhode Island to the Caribbean."

Clara looked confused. "Why doesn't Señor Rich Person take his boat to the Caribbean himself?"

Flora said, "It could be a she."

Clara pursed her lips. "Fine, Señora Rich Person."

She shrugged. "I guess it's a thing. They're too busy or something, so they hire people to sail their boats from here to their homes in the islands."

"You get *paid* to sail someone else's fancy boat? How much?"

Flora said, "I have no idea. But I want that job."

Flora felt her phone buzz. It was a text from her mother. "¿Dónde estás?"

She stepped out of the boat. "It's my mom. I better get home."

"Me too," Clara said.

They walked home, talking the whole way about boats and how they couldn't wait until they were old enough to take a year off of school and get paid cold, hard cash to lounge about on a boat all day. Being in the fifth grade was fun. But being teenagers together was going to be *everything*.

CHAPTER 2

Flora's House

The brown shingled cottage where Flora lived with her parents and older sister looked almost like every other house in their little seaside village. But what Flora liked about her house was that there was a secret behind it. When you went into the house and through the back door, there was a stone path that led to another brown shingled house, one that was much bigger. That house belonged to her uncle Rogelio and his family—and *that* house had a private path to the beach.

Sunday dinners were always at Flora's house, even if it was smaller. The kitchen was cozier and it spilled onto a patio that they used nearly year round. That November afternoon was no different, Flora's mother calling out, "¡Maylin! ¡Flora! Necesito su ayuda."

Maylin was Flora's older sister. She was awful. Flora was convinced that if they ever performed surgery on her only sibling, they would find out that there was a hard, cold rock where Maylin's heart should be. To say Maylin was mean was a gross understatement. She was stingy. And a tattletale. And of course, Maylin was their parents' favorite. Flora wondered what you called someone who was the teacher's pet, but with parents. "Parents' pet" didn't sound right. But there had to be a word. Whatever it was, Maylin was it.

Flora's sister came into the kitchen and said, "Pero Mami, no puedo. I just painted my nails."

Her mother said, "Okay, Flora, you'll be my helper today." Flora couldn't believe it. Maylin was fourteen going on full-blown diva. She was a genius at doing as little around the house as humanly possible.

This time, however, Flora wasn't having it. "Mami, her *nails*? Really?" Then, just to prove that there was hateration where her heart should be, Maylin winked at Flora as she floated up the stairs to her room.

* * *

Flora's mother stood at the kitchen island, chopping potatoes.

"Come, sit," she said, gesturing to the high-back stool next to the island.

"What are you making?" Flora asked, feeling thankful all of a sudden for the time alone with her mother.

Damaris Delfina LeFevre was a cardiothoracic surgeon, which meant she operated on hearts. She went to bed early during the week and spent long hours at the hospital. The weekends were usually all for family

time. But Maylin was turning fifteen that spring and so every Saturday, it seemed, Flora's mother was tied up with quinceañera planning.

To be fair to Maylin, the whole quince setup had built-in telenovela level drama. The birthday girl is attended to by a court of fourteen friends and family members—seven damas and seven chambelanes. The court all wore matching outfits, there was a DJ, choreographed dances, catering, gift bags for guests. It was a *thing*.

"What are you making for tonight?" Flora asked

as her mother handed her a bowl of meat that Flora began to roll into tiny meatballs. "Besides these albóndigas?"

"I thought I'd keep it simple," her mother said. "Just tapas: patatas bravas, croquetas, albóndigas, a cheese and meat plate, and an arroz negro with seafood."

Flora grinned. "Mami, your definition of simple and my definition of simple are not the same."

Her mother said, "I like cooking. It relaxes me."

Flora looked at her mother and asked, "Mami, does your work stress you out?"

Her mother lined the perfectly cut potatoes on a tray and paused before she answered. "Yes and no. It's delicate work, and that's stressful. But créeme Floracita, there is nothing like holding a human heart in your hand. It's the most beautiful thing in the world."

Flora thought for a second and said, "But when you're holding the heart in your hand, it's covered in blood, right?"

Her mother nodded.

Flora shook her head. "That's just disgusting."

Her mother laughed and shook her head. "Es un

milagro, but I can totally see how you might find it a little disgusting."

At that moment, Maylin the Maleficent walked into the kitchen.

"What's disgusting?" she said, reaching for a bag of tortilla chips on the counter.

"Your face," Flora whispered, smiling sweetly.

"Mami!" Maylin called out plaintively. "Did you hear that? Did you hear how she talks to me?"

"Kidding," Flora said as she jumped off the barstool.

But as she went to the kitchen sink to wash her hands, she felt a swell of pride.

By her count, the day's score was Flora-1. Maylin-0.

CHAPTER 3

La Familia

It was Flora's job to set the table for family suppers. She placed each dish on the long oak dining table in front of the door that led out to the garden. Her father made that table, as he had made almost everything in their house. He liked to say he was a carpenter, but she thought of him as an artist. He designed all kinds of furniture and his work was so popular that just the year before, he'd been able to open his own shop on Canal Street, the main street in town.

Flora ran her finger along the pale wood grain. There was something about her father's furniture that felt even more beautiful to her, as if he had made it just for her.

As she placed the forks on top of the navy-blue linen napkins, she could hear the family and friends arriving through the back door of the house. There was her tío Rogelio—tall and handsome, with the same dark skin and wavy hair as her mother. There was her uncle's husband, her tío Luca—he was a former ballet dancer and everything about the way he moved was smooth and elegant. Luca was holding their baby girl. The baby was named Damaris Delfina, after Flora's mother. But everyone called the baby Delfina or Fina, for short.

Next to arrive was her grandmother. Abuela lived nearby in a town called Mystic. Flora ran up to her and gave her a squeeze. Even when it was freezing out, her grandmother smelled like summer, like agua de pipa and fresh cut ginger and how in the summer, in Rhode Island, everywhere you looked there were trees that sprayed white and yellow blossoms across bright green lawns.

"Bienvenida, Abuela," she said, taking in her scent.

Her grandmother pulled her away and looked at her in disbelief. "Ay niña, you're almost as tall as me!"

It was true. At ten, Flora was nearly as tall as her grandmother. But as she pointed out: "Abuela, I hate to be the one to break it to you, but you're also super short."

Her abuela puffed out her chest and said, "¡No me digas! When I stand on the ladder that is my heart, I'm six feet tall."

"Oh Abuela, you're so silly," Flora said, kissing her on the cheek.

The door creaked open again and the kitchen filled with more guests. There was her tía Janet and her husband, Tío Aarón. They weren't really her aunt and uncle, but she'd been taught to call every adult from Panama aunt or uncle. Flora didn't mind—she liked the idea of being from a place so small and tightly knit that anyone who lived there could be considered family.

Abuela had brought along the guy she called "my gentleman friend." His name was Mr. Carter. Since he wasn't from Panama, Flora's mother said it was okay to call him Mr. Carter and so she did.

Mr. Carter sat in the living room with Flora's father, examining a piece of wood that Papá was crafting into a side table.

"Flora! Maylin! Cozy, cozy!" her mother called out.

Flora knew that meant she and her sister were to add the four folding chairs that were kept in the basement to the dining room table.

Maylin called out, "Tía Janet is braiding my hair, can't Flora do it?"

Flora didn't even wait for her mother to respond "No hay problema." Sometimes Flora wondered if Maylin was not actually her sister but a real life princess that her parents had been charged to raise, like Princess Leia in the Obi Wan Kenobi series. It was like she could Jedi mind trick everyone around her. After she'd squeezed the folding chairs in between the wooden chairs with the cloud-gray cushions her father had made, Flora went to the cabinet with the dishes. She counted out ten bone-white plates and ten blue ombre napkins.

Her mother brought a tray of patatas bravas to the table and looked at Flora's handiwork approvingly. "So good," she said, kissing her on the forehead. "Flora, tú eres formidable."

The guests all poured into the dining room and Flora sat between her dad and her tío Luca.

As they passed serving platters back and forth, her abuela asked, "Ay, Flora, dime. ¿Cómo está tu español?"

Flora shrugged. "Pretty good. Tomo clases cada sábado."

Maylin looked at her scornfully. "And yet, your accent remains tan feo."

Flora flinched. It was true, her accent was a little different from the rest of the family's. She'd never be truly bilingual, but at least she tried. It wasn't her fault that she'd been born in Boston and raised in Rhode Island. Just because her accent wasn't flawless didn't mean it was ugly.

Nobody criticized Maylin for being so hurtful. Rather her tía Janet just encouraged her by asking, "And Maylin, how goes planning for your quince?"

Flora wanted to do one of those slow-motion dives across the table to stop the words from coming out of her tía's mouth. Once Maylin started talking about her quince, there would be no way to put the quincezilla back into the bottle. But it was too late.

"Gracias, Tía," Maylin said, as if she were on stage and someone had just handed her a big, shiny gold award. "I don't have to tell you, but planning a quince is a full-time job. There are so many damas and chambelanes to dress and instruct what to do. One of my damas has already missed two dance classes. I called her up and said, 'Chica, if you think I'm going to let you embarrass me at my quince, you have another thing coming.'"

For the rest of dinner, it was the Maylin show, and Flora wished there were a trapdoor beneath her seat, a way to escape the room that had, all of a sudden, started to feel *Alice in Wonderland* small.

Finally, when the platters were filled with nothing but crumbs and the remnants of fresh herbs that her mother had used to season each dish, she was sprung free. Her father said, "Flora, help me clear the table, querida."

Flora nodded and collected the plates as Maylin pattered on. "I've had no luck finding a dress. Tú sabes, tengo un estilo muy refinado and I don't want to just recycle a poofy prom dress the way so many girls do."

As Flora stood side by side in the kitchen with her father, he said, "It's not easy being in the middle."

Flora was confused. "What do you mean?"

"Well, Maylin is the oldest."

Flora said, "She's also self-centered más que nada. Continue."

Her father said, "You have Maylin on one hand and now Delfina is the baby."

Flora was going to be starting middle school in a year. She certainly wasn't worried about not being the baby of the family.

Her father was nothing if not perceptive. He said, "I know I'm not explaining it perfectly, but I guess what I'm trying to say is that when I was a kid, I felt stuck in the middle. My brother Ben was older and a soccer star. My little brother Dimitry was younger but he was a musical prodigy from the age of four. It took me a while to find my thing. But I also came to realize that there's kind of a magic to being in the middle. I was surrounded by a lot of love."

Listening to the orchestra of voices coming from the dining room, Flora knew her father wasn't wrong. She did feel surrounded by love.

Then Maylin called out from the dining room, "Flora, bring us some water."

Her father gave her a look that said "Cálmate."

She wanted to take the jug of water out of the fridge and slam it on the table. But instead she handed it to her father, who took it into the dining room.

She opened the calendar on her father's iPad and did some quick math. Only 912 days until Maylin went to college. Then she would be the only kid/teenager in the house. She could hardly wait. It was going to be awesome.

CHAPTER 4

Clara's House

Flora and Clara both liked drawing—which they were good at. And skateboarding—they could only do one or two tricks, but they liked to tape each other on the half-pipe and record voice-overs like they were smashing it in a big fancy competition. Every Saturday, to help blow off steam after Spanish school, they would take their boards down to the skate park and practice their moves. They were the only girls who ever showed up, which made them feel a little lonely, but also kind of cool.

At the skate park, Clara put on her helmet and did a quick flip on the half-pipe. Flora's mother made her wear a helmet, elbow pads, knee pads and wrist guards. "Why don't you just wrap my whole body in bubble wrap while you're at it?" Flora groaned every time.

But her mother didn't seem to get that she was joking. "Don't tempt me, *niña*," she said, "I just might."

Even though her mother wasn't at the park, Flora dutifully put all the pads on. Clara laughed. "All you need is a pillow wrapped around your belly and you would be like totally protected."

Flora looked annoyed. "Don't laugh, Clara."

Clara said, "Your mom is nowhere to be found. You look like you're shipping yourself special delivery halfway around the world."

Flora shook her head, "Uh-uh. The day I don't wear these things is the day my mom decides to do an unannounced drive by—or send Maylin to spy on me."

"Can you come over to my house for a snack when we're done?" Clara asked.

Flora texted her mother and gave the thumbs-up when she quickly got the response saying okay.

Flora often thought her house was the unofficial Panamanian embassy of New England. In contrast, she could count on Clara's house to not only be a Maylin-free zone, but to be a bastion of peace and quiet. Clara's house was rarely crowded and hardly

ever loud. Clara's parents were from Argentina, which meant their food was a little different from Panamanian, but equally delicious.

In the notes app on her phone, Flora kept a running list of all the cool things about Clara. She was proud of the list even though whenever she offered to show it to Clara, Clara just laughed and said, "Flora LeFevre, the only cool thing about me is that I get to hang out with you."

Clara was that way—always humble and kind. Which reminded Flora—she needed to add those to her list.

CLARA COOL THING #1

Clara was an only child, which meant she had no big sister and no adorable baby cousin who might, in the middle of a delicious dinner, drop a stinky diaper so big that you could—and would—lose your appetite.

Once, Clara told Flora, "I know Maylin is the worst. But sometimes being an only kid gets lonely."

This was something Flora had a hard time believing.

"I live five blocks away," she said. "If you get lonely, just call me. I'll be right over."

Clara had not made one of her trademark funny faces then. She just looked at Flora seriously and said, "That's not what I meant, Flora la Fresca."

Flora asked her, "Well, what do you mean?"

Clara shrugged and said, "Forget about it."

Flora was quiet then. As much as she hated having a truly self-absorbed older sister, she did love that her uncles lived right next door and her abuela was never far away. Her house might feel like a zoo sometimes, but it was her zoo. She knew that Clara's abuelos lived in Buenos Aires and only visited once a year. She couldn't imagine seeing Abuela just once a year.

CLARA COOL THING #2

Clara's mother, whom Flora called Tía Mariana, was a cartographer, which is a fancy word for mapmaker. Clara told Flora, "You'd think there wouldn't be a huge demand for new maps. But it turns out, there is!"

Clara's mother worked from home in a beautiful art studio with three ginormous skylights and filled with easels, a big artsy computer screen, colored pencils and paints. Flora sometimes thought that when she grew up, all she wanted was to have an apartment that was just like that studio. She wouldn't even need a kitchen. Clara's mother had a little kettle and fridge in the studio and sometimes when they came over after school, she made Clara and Flora big steaming mugs of ramen noodles with that kettle, and it was the best after-school snack ever.

Mariana drew maps for textbook publishers, but she also made maps of cities with little drawings that symbolized all the best places to visit and eat and shop. She sold those maps online and they were even featured in magazines.

Sometimes, after they were done with their homework, Clara's mom would show them how to sketch faces or how to use different kinds of watercolors. Both Flora and Clara had become pretty good artists. They always got an A in art. In fourth grade, Clara had come in first at the school art fair with her model of a house with an entirely green roof. She'd made the roof out of real moss and written a whole report on the environmental benefits of green roofs—how they improved air quality and helped reduce the carbon footprint of the home.

Flora had done a portrait of her parents in traditional Panamanian clothes—her mother in a brightly colored pollera dress and her father in a montuno shirt and a straw hat. She'd come in second in the art contest and the girls had celebrated by going out for boba tea in town.

CLARA COOL THING #3
(SPOILER ALERT: IT'S REALLY COOL.)

The third thing on Flora's list was the coolest thing of all. Clara's house had a pool. *Inside* the house. The first time Flora saw it, she and Clara had already been friends for weeks. Which was good because Flora would've never wanted Clara to think she was her friend just to get access to a pool.

They were well into second grade when Clara first invited Flora over for a play date. She said, "Bring your suit, we can go swimming."

Flora put her hand on Clara's forehead and said, "It's November, loca! The water is *freezing*."

Clara said, "I know. We have a pool."

Flora didn't get it. "Chica, do you know how cold it is outside?"

Clara looked like she was getting frustrated. "Ya, yo sé. It's an indoor pool." Those were two words Flora had never heard put together—*indoor* and *pool*. But it turned out, Clara wasn't loca after all. In the back of *her* brown shingled cottage, where a lot of people had a sunporch, Clara's family had a pool. On the inside.

Clara's dad, Joaquín, designed pools for rich people. So when they moved into the house, he designed one for them. The pool was long and thin. Clara's dad called it a lap pool, and it had the most beautiful black tile that sparkled when the sun hit it just right.

Every once in a while, after they'd had a swim on a cold winter day, Flora would say to Clara, "Are you sure you're not rich?"

Clara would say, "I don't think so. I'm pretty sure my parents would tell me if we were loaded."

But the last time Flora asked her, Clara said, "Maybe we're rich adjacent."

Flora laughed and said, "What does *that* mean?"

"It means we're close to it. So, like my dad designs pools for rich people. So he's adjacent to their richness and I'm adjacent to him."

Flora sat wrapped in a big beach towel next to Clara, their legs dangling in the heated pool as they looked out on the garden, where every branch looked wintry and bare.

"Oh, I get it," Flora said. "So I'm monster adjacent because my bedroom is right next to Maylin's."

"Exactly," Clara said, nodding.

Flora said, "Did I tell you her new thing is refusing to help with chores because her nails are painted?"

Clara looked at her nails, which were short and unpainted like Flora's.

"Does that actually work?"

Flora nodded.

Clara shook her head. "*Insoportable.*"

That was one of their favorite Spanish words. It meant, incredibly, you-had-to-see-it-to-believe-it, so bad it was practically criminal, unbearable, and unjust.

Flora thought again about how lucky it was that Clara was an only child. She said, "If it gets worse and she goes full-tilt quince loca, can I come and live with you?"

Clara nodded. "Pues, tengo que preguntar a los padres, but it would be totally cool with me."

CHAPTER 5

How'd We Get Kicked Off the Nice List?

On the first Sunday in December, Flora went over to Clara's to swim. Swimming in Clara's pool was always fun, but swimming when there was snow on the ground was always an extra thrill. When Flora got home and saw that Clara was FaceTiming her, she answered the call and said, "¡Hola Clarita! What did I forget?"

Clara's hair was still wet from the pool and the skin around her eyes looked red and sore, like she'd rubbed her hands in poison ivy, then rubbed her eyes.

"Chica, what's wrong?" Flora asked, worried.

"It's my . . ." Clara could barely get the words out. Flora had never seen her so upset. "Take a deep breath, Clara," she said. Flora's mother said that when people came to the hospital, the first thing they forgot to do was breathe. So she was always reminding them, "Take a deep breath."

Clara inhaled and exhaled audibly. "It's my mother . . . She got a job in California and we're moving after New Year's."

Flora heard the words come out of Clara's mouth but they sounded far away, like when they used to try to make walkie-talkies out of tin cans and string. She was sure she didn't hear Clara right.

"I think I still have water in my ears from the pool," Flora said hopefully, tapping one ear toward the ground and then the other. She knew she didn't, but the gesture felt comforting.

"It's true," Clara said.

They stood there, silently. Staring at each other over the phone. Flora didn't know what to say. She'd never had a problem of this magnitude before (*magnitude* had been on their weekly spelling quiz at the start of fifth grade). Before, she could spell the word, but now she felt how big the word was, the *magnitude* of Clara moving away was like a giant construction wrecking ball had knocked a crater-sized hole in the center of her gut.

* * *

Flora's dad loved to watch old-school crime shows, especially the ones with a gazillion episodes and the ticking clock theme. Flora noticed that when things went wrong, it was very important to pay attention to the time. On the show, people were always saying things like, "He walked in the bar, it must've been around seven p.m." And "She was never late for work, so by ten a.m., I started to worry."

On her last birthday, Flora's parents gave her a pink leather book with a lock and a key. She'd never used it because she hated the color pink. But she also never thought she had anything that important to say. But now the unimaginable was happening. Things were getting bad and all indications were that they were only going to get worse.

She opened the sickly pink book and began to write: *Clara's mother got a job in California and the whole family is moving after New Year's.*

She added, although it hardly seemed necessary: *My life is ruined and this is about to be the worst Christmas ever.*

Then she closed the book and wiped away her small but steady stream of tears.

✳ ✳ ✳

The next day, after school, Flora and Clara met up at their favorite hangout place, Bruce Lee Boba, to think up a plan.

Normally, the photos of the iconic martial arts star would cheer them up, but the idea that Clara was moving, all the way to the other side of the country, was bad news on the level that even Bruce Lee and his fists of fury couldn't fix.

"Maybe my parents would let me come live with you so I can finish out the school year here," Clara offered.

Flora's heart leaped. "If you lived with me, it would be like having a sister and a best friend rolled into one."

"I like the way you think," Clara said, smiling at the idea. Then she slurped the bubbles at the bottom of her glass.

"Why, thank you."

"I'll ask my dad as soon as he gets home," Clara said.

"Me too," Flora said.

It went without saying that for a plan like this to work they needed to start with the fathers. Latina moms had a reputation for being tough to crack, and the girls' mothers weren't exceptions to the rule.

When Flora got home, her father was in the kitchen. "Your mother's had a long day at the hospital," he said. "I thought I'd make dinner. Tacos work for you?"

Perfect, Flora thought. *I've got him cornered.*

"Papá," she began. "Clara really doesn't want to start a new school in the middle of the year. Would it be okay if she lived with us so she could finish out the fifth grade here, in Westerly?"

Her father didn't even turn around from the pile of fresh tortillas he was baking in the oven. "Of course. Clara's always welcome here. She's like family."

Flora jumped up. It had been surprisingly easy. Could it really be that easy? "Thank you, Papá," she said, trying to control her excitement lest she jinx the whole deal. "You're the best."

He called out after her, "It's really up to Clara's parents, though."

But Flora couldn't see how that was going to be a big deal. Clara's parents were ruining their lives. They *had* to say yes.

Flora went up to her room and texted Clara:

My dad says you can live with us (!!!)

Clara texted back a GIF of a dancing cat.

Flora looked around her room. There was plenty of space for a second bed. Maybe she and Clara could even get bunk beds. She'd always wanted bunk beds. She didn't want Clara to move, but if she could stay with them for the rest of the school year, they might be able to squeeze in just enough fun to make it all bearable.

Flora tried to get her homework done, but she couldn't. It was all too exciting. So she opened her tablet and decided to watch her favorite Studio Ghibli movie until it was dinner time.

She was halfway through *Howl's Moving Castle* when she got an alert. It was Clara:

We're on our way to your house. My mom called your mom.

Then a second message:

It's not good.

For all her fresca ways, Flora hadn't gotten in very much trouble before. So when she heard the doorbell ring a few minutes later, she was more curious than scared. Clara's family was already moving to California. What could be more *not good* than that?

But when she came down the stairs and saw Clara's family and her parents sitting in the fancy living room, the one with the big vase of fake flowers and the off-white couches that no one was ever allowed to sit on, she knew that things were serious.

Her mother looked tired and mad.

Clara's mother looked frustrated and mad.

The dads looked like if they could make a quick escape to the basement to watch soccer and avoid whatever was coming next, they would.

Clara sat crisscross applesauce in front of the bay window. She patted the floor and indicated that Flora should sit next to her. Flora's mother sighed and said, "Mariana, do you want to start?" Clearly the mothers had been plotting against them before the girls even knew they were in a battle.

"Sure," Mariana said. "Look, chicas. I know that this move is hard for you to take. If I could change the timing, I would, but I cannot."

Her voice caught in her throat then, and Flora thought she might cry. Mariana took a deep breath and continued, "It's hard when something that is good news for you is bad news for the people you love. But Joaquín and I think that in the long term, this is a huge opportunity for our whole family."

Clara looked at her mother without a dash of sympathy and said, "If it's good news for you, then just leave me here."

Her mother shook her head and said, "Eso no va a pasar."

Flora jumped in to defend the plan she and Clara had. "But Tía Mariana, my dad said it was okay."

Flora's father looked at Clara's parents apologetically. "Lo siento, amigos. Ustedes saben. She misunderstood my comments. All I meant was that Clara will always be welcome in our home."

Mariana sighed. "And Flora will always be welcome in our home. Tal vez, when they're a bit older, they can even spend some of their summer vacations together."

Clara was not appeased. She said, "But why not let me finish the school year here?"

Mariana's voice turned from weary to forceful. "Because you are ten years old, Clara Beatriz Lucía Ocampo Londra." Flora knew it was bad then because Mariana had used all five of the names on Clara's birth certificate. It was like both of their mothers had taken the same course for Latina Moms on Discipline and Expressing Abject Disappointment.

Clara started to cry, the kind of crying you did when you fell off the jungle gym and you hit the ground so hard and fast that everything hurt. Flora put her arms around her friend, felt the sleeve of her t-shirt go from dry to wet in seconds. Then she looked at the parents accusingly. "Do you see what you've *done*?"

Flora's mother snapped to her feet. "Flora, ven conmigo a la cocina."

Flora followed her reluctantly to the kitchen as Clara fell into her father's arms.

"Flora, you have to stop," her mother said, her voice as sharp as the special set of knives she used for cooking. "You are making a hard situation worse. You are not in charge here. The Ocampos are. Stop making suggestions. Stop acting like you can control any of this."

Flora thought this was wildly unfair, but she said nothing.

"Do you hear me?" her mother asked, her voice thick with irritation.

Flora nodded.

"I'm going to need to hear actual words," her mother said.

"Te escucho," Flora whispered. On the list of things that were the absolute worst, her mother being mad—like really mad—at her was definitely in Flora's top five.

"And?"

"And I'm sorry." Flora let the untrue words come out of her mouth."

"Don't apologize to me. Apologize to Tía Mariana and Tío Joaquín for being so bad-mannered."

Flora nodded again.

Back in the living room, Clara's tears had slowed down and Flora sat on the edge of the leather armchair next to her. She looked at Clara's parents and said, "Lo siento. I'm sorry for being rude."

Mariana said, "Ay Flora, it's okay. This isn't going to be easy. But at least we have the holidays together. Why don't you both focus on enjoying the time you have together instead of trying to stop the inevitable?"

"Okay," Flora said softly.

Clara shrugged, defeated, and said, "Okay."

Clara and her parents stayed for dinner. Under normal circumstances, that would have been a treat.

Plus, they were having tacos. Flora's dad's tacos, with the homemade tortillas and special sauces, were better than any restaurant within driving distance of Westerly—everyone said so.

But Flora could barely taste her food and when Clara and her parents left, she went straight to her room.

She took out her diary and opened the girly pink pages to record the evidence that she had gathered that day: *December 2nd, 7:15 p.m. Christmas is canceled and my life is ruined.*

CHAPTER 6

Grumpy Elves

The next day, the girls knew there was nothing to do but meet up at The Cooked Goose, a little café near the waterfront where they went sometimes for french fries and Cherry Cokes. As they waited for their usual order, they discussed the previous evening's events.

"I know my mother is a total Wendy," Flora said. "But I expected more from your parents."

Wendys were what Flora and Clara called grown-ups who were like the character in Peter Pan, growing up and forgetting all about how cool it was to fly and how awesome it was to be a kid in general.

Flora took out her phone and counted the weeks. "We've got five weeks," she said. Clara took her keychain out of her bag and held it like a stethoscope to her own heart.

"Doctor," Clara said, in a very not-serious pretend-serious voice, "I give the patient five weeks."

Flora smiled. "We've got to make it count."

Clara nodded. "We'll spend every weekend together."

"And we'll do eight thousand sleepovers."

Clara grinned. "Your math is, like, really bad. You can't do eight thousand sleepovers in a month."

Flora shrugged. "Einstein said the only reason for time is so that everything doesn't happen at once."

"You're absolutely right, my dear Fresca. We've got to beat time. We've got to make everything happen at once!"

That weekend, after Spanish Saturday school, the girls went over to Clara's house. Every year, they made Christmas presents for their family and this year, with all the bad news, they were a little behind.

"The parents all deserve lumps of coal," Clara said as they laid out their art supplies on the kitchen table.

"Maybe that's what we should get them," Flora said, only half kidding. "Pedazos de carbón. I bet my uncle could help me find some at the quarry."

Clara held an invisible magnifying glass to her eye and did her best Enola Holmes impersonation. "That is a *capital* plan, Flora la Fresca, but . . ."

"But . . ."

"I don't want them to say that we ruined Christmas," Clara said reluctantly.

Flora took a deep breath. "*We* didn't ruin Christmas, they did."

This was one of her tareas as Clara's best friend. It wasn't enough just to take Clara's side in moments of conflict; Flora felt like it was her job to be honest in a way that Clara could count on—like Wonder Woman's Lasso of Truth.

Clara's mother came into the kitchen and said, "Who wants chocolate a la taza?"

Flora wanted to say no. It felt important to not let the grown-ups think everything was okay. But then Clara said, "Gracias, Mami."

When Mariana put the steaming mugs of thick, creamy chocolate in front of them, Clara kissed her mother on the cheek. Flora could hardly believe it. Was Clara not *devastated* about the move? What was up with the besitos as if everything was okay?

Flora sipped her chocolate and ran her finger across the thick, cottony watercolor paper.

"I might as well start with Maylin the Malevolent," she said. "How about I draw her with a crown spiked with thorns and fangs that drip blood down her ruby-red cape?"

"You can't," Clara said, sounding mature and reasonable in a way that Flora did not really appreciate.

"Fine," Flora said, "how about this?"

She did a quick sketch of Maylin in a T-shirt with the word *Princesa* stenciled across it.

"I like it," Clara said. "It's subtle."

Flora thought, *Since when is subtle our thing?* But she didn't say it. She wanted to make these weeks with Clara as perfect as possible. Even though she could feel all the ways in which things were already changing.

Clara said, "I'm going to do dream house sketches for my gifts. This one is for your mom."

She sketched the outline of a modern beach house. Within minutes, Flora could see the house, a path to the beach, and the waves on the shore. Clara's hand was so sure, she didn't even pick up her eraser once.

"You're so good," Flora said with admiration as she began another drawing, this time of her father's face.

"Your mother talks a lot about someday getting a house in Bocas del Toro," Clara said, holding up the drawing. "So I thought it would be cool to do something that's a beach house but a little different. My mom has a book about Moorish architecture, so I drew these curved archways. And once the drawing is done, I'll hand paint the tile work with oils and little teeny-tiny paintbrushes. I'll get my mom to help me." Flora stared at the drawing and thought about how easily the line could also be erased and both memory and the future would disappear with Clara's move.

"Do you want more hot chocolate?" Clara asked.

Flora nodded.

Her friend mixed the thick, creamy mixture on the stove, adding in just a little milk to thin it out.

When their cups were refilled, the two girls sat together looking out of the skylight in the kitchen at the dark, gray winter sky.

It was only four in the afternoon, but it would be dark soon. And the shortness of the days reminded them both of the shortness of the time they had left together.

Flora took a sip from her cup and asked her friend, "Are you nervous, Clarita? Are you nervous about going to a new school? Making new friends?"

She shrugged. "I'm pretty committed to the fact that the next six months are going to be extraordinarily difficult."

"Lo siento," Flora said, feeling as sorry as she sounded. "We've just got to make the most of the time we have left."

Clara smiled and said, "We'll do better than that. We'll bend time and space like the superheroes we are."

CHAPTER 7

Maps

When Flora went home that night, she found herself staring at a magnet on the fridge. It featured a quote from the poet Maya Angelou and it said, "When you know better, do better." It was one of her mother's favorite quotes, but it had never really meant a lot to Flora before then. Staring at the magnet, Flora knew, with a certainty that started at the top of her head and went to the bottom of her toes, that she needed to let Clara know that even though she didn't want her to move, she didn't want to ruin Clara's move. What could she do to remind Clara of her when she was so far away?

She spent the next two weeks working on a secret project, inspired by the fancy maps that Clara's mom drew—an illustrated guide to Clara's soon-to-be hometown of San Francisco. For her birthday, Mariana had given Flora a roll of butcher block paper. "It's better if you just draw and draw, and not think too much about it." Flora used that paper for Clara's map—trying not to think about how good Clara's sketches were the first time around, and just letting herself draw on a long scroll of the paper, then feeling the freedom to ball it up, throw it away, and start again.

Each night, after dinner, she did drawings of famous places Clara might want to visit—from the cable cars and the Presidio to the Golden Gate Bridge and Fisherman's Wharf.

With her dad's help, Flora looked up all the best places to eat in San Francisco where Clara was going to live. She included the best places for tacos (Clara's favorite), pizza (Tío Joaquín's favorite), and ice cream (everybody's other favorite).

In the last free spot of the folded map, Flora drew a picture of her and Flora in scuba gear swimming with the otters. Clara loved otters. When she was done, Flora showed the map—which spread out the length of her entire dining table—to her parents.

"Flora la Fresca, eres una maravilla. You're so creative, just like your father," her mother said, and Flora could tell by the way her eyes took it all in that she really meant it.

Her father squeezed her shoulder and said, "You're really quite the artist, Florita. I ought to hire you to do some art for my store."

Maylin walked by and looked over the entire map without saying a word. Flora could feel her whole body tense up. Why did Maylin have to show up and ruin the moment? Her sister looked carefully at the map, from one end of the table to the other. "It's not horrible," she said, finally. "If I weren't having my quince invites done by a professional, I would, maybe, give you a shot."

Flora could hardly believe it. Maylin was being . . . *nice?* Unsure of what to say, she just mumbled, "Uh, thanks."

Maylin rolled her eyes. "Uh, you're welcome." Then she walked away.

Flora turned to her parents and said, "When I look at all of this, I actually feel a little jealous. I know

Clara is going to a new school and that's got to be scary. But she'll have all these cool places to visit when they get settled. She's moving to this big city and I've only ever lived in this little town."

"Be happy for her, querida," her father said, giving her shoulder another squeeze.

"De acuerdo," her mother said. "Who knows? I've got so many unused vacation days, maybe next summer we can go for a visit."

Flora said, "Okay, gracias Mami." If she said what she was thinking, that *everything* good in her life was ending and her parents had no idea how lonely life was going to be without Clara, she knew what her parents would say. "Don't be so dramatic, Flora."

But that was the thing they didn't understand. She was only dramatic because her life was filled with drama. And Clara moving was the worst kind of earth-shattering drama she'd ever faced.

CHAPTER 8

The BFF-ometer

Every New Year's Eve, Clara's parents had a big party. There were homemade empanadas and a big barbecue. There must have been a hundred people between the crowds that filled every room in the house.

It was always Flora and Clara's favorite night of the year. But as she got dressed for the party, Flora couldn't help but think. If only she could stop time. If she could make it so that the clock never struck twelve and it wasn't a new year, then maybe, just maybe, everything would stay the same. Clara wouldn't be moving to California. And the days ahead would just be like the days behind them.

January was heavy jacket weather in Rhode Island. But the Ocampos had an outdoor fireplace and a giant

Argentinian-style grill and the backyard was full of New England born and New England raised Latinos who had gotten used to the cold.

Clara's father commanded the grill and her mother shuffled trays in and out of the house: platters of asparagus and porcini mushrooms, platters of sliced beef, pork, chicken, and chorizo.

Clara and Flora were in Clara's room, staring at the ominous-looking suitcases that were already packed.

Flora's mother knocked on the door. "¡Hola, Clara!" she said. "I have a regalito for you."

She handed Clara a box. It was a ginormous Lego City Lunar Research Base complete with a VIPER rover, a moon buggy, and six astronaut figures. Clara loved Lego.

"Come on, Mamá," Flora said. "It's our last New Year's together, we can't do Lego."

Flora's mother looked hurt. "I thought you could use a distraction tonight."

Clara said, "Tía Jasmine, I love it. Thank you."

Flora rolled her eyes.

"¡Flora!" Her mother began. "No seas . . ."

Flora knew what her mother was about to say. *No seas tan grosera.* Don't be so rude.

But her mother didn't finish her sentence. She stopped, then kissed each girl on her forehead and admitted, "It's a tough night."

She turned to Flora and said, "Tonight, I let it slide."

After her mother left, Flora said, "It's a kajillion bajillion pieces. We'll never get it done tonight."

Clara's eyes lit up. "We'll stay up all night, Flora la Fresca. It will be our impossible dream. Like Don Quixote chasing windmills."

Flora groaned as quietly as she could.

The summer before, in Saturday Spanish school, they had read the kids' version of the Cervantes novel. It had been a rare moment of disagreement between Flora and Clara. Clara loved the story of Don Quixote, the hapless dreamer who sets off on a quest to become a knight. Flora thought Don Quixote was a lughead and a bully who should have left poor Sancho Panza alone.

Clara looked at Flora. "I heard that groan."

She came over and put her arms around Flora. "I really think we have only two choices. No, I tell a lie, I believe we have three choices."

Flora sat on the floor in Clara's beautiful room. There was a big four-poster bed and a built-in Murphy bed for sleepovers, two cotton candy pink wing chairs, and a long table for puzzles that looked out onto the backyard.

"I'm listening," Flora said.

Clara got up, dashed into the closet, and returned with a black cape and a cane. She pointed to the bathroom door. "Behind door number one, there is the choice to spend the night sobbing and feeling sorry for ourselves."

Flora smiled. "A little emo, but I like it."

Clara spun around and her cape fluttered behind her. Flora wondered, *Where am I ever going to find a friend with that kind of style? Nowhere and not ever.*

Clara said, "Behind door number two"—she pointed to the closet—"is a night of empanadas, Lego, and playing all of our favorite songs as long as we like."

"Can I DJ?" Flora asked hopefully.

"You are—always and forever—the DJ." Clara pointed at Flora, then spun around and pointed out the speakers.

"Okay," Flora said. "That one seems less emotionally draining than door number one. But what is door number three?"

Clara turned the lights out in the room, something she did often. Then Clara turned on the giant flashlight her mom kept under the puzzle table and pointed to the backyard. "The last option, Flora la Fresca, door number three, is we throw ourselves onto my papá's grill and spend the rest of our lives as tasty, tasty BBQ."

Flora raised one eyebrow, then another. "Come on, Clarita, our parents are not going to become cannibals."

Clara said, "That's where your mind goes? Not to the burn of the flames?"

Flora looked at her friend and said, "You're weird."

Clara smiled and said, "How about we go to the moon with this Lego set?"

"I've got one more idea," Flora said. "What if we make our own game? We can call it the BFF-ometer. We can create a simple program on your computer."

"I love it already," Clara said, turning her laptop on.

The BFF-ometer was a test they would create to help them find worthy replacement friends after Clara left. They created the BFF program using a simple coding tool called Scratch. Question #1 was, of course, "Can you use Scratch?" Clara and Flora thought this was very funny. But it would also be telling. None of the other girls in their class could work even the most basic programs. The girls had made a rule a long time ago, a long time meaning back in third grade when they made their first pocket chip console. The rule was they only hung out with girls who knew how to code or ones who were willing to learn.

Question #2: "Do you speak Spanish?" Whenever they didn't want the other kids to understand them, Clara and Flora spoke in Spanish, or more accurately, Spanglish. For Christmas, Flora's mom had gotten them matching T-shirts that said: *Pero, like* . . . Because that's what they always said as in: "Sí, Philip Pullman es el mejor en todo el mundo, pero, like . . . you can't sleep on Rick Riordan."

Clara said, "I don't mind if my new California

friend doesn't speak Spanish, but she's got to speak something other than English."

Flora said, "Exactamundo. I don't want to be friends with someone who isn't even *trying* to learn another language."

So they amended the Scratch quiz to have a default response if the answer to the question was no. You could still get one point out of two if you were willing to learn Spanish or if you spoke another language.

Even though Flora and Clara called their quiz the BFF-ometer, they didn't exactly mean that. They would always be each other's BFFs, because the last F in BFF stands for *forever*. But California was a long, long way from Rhode Island, and they were trying to be *realistic*, which is what grown-ups said whenever they wanted you to take bad news without a single solitary complaint. When Flora found out Clara was moving to California, she'd asked her parents if they could move to California too. Flora's father sighed and said, "Come on Flora, be *realistic*." The BFF-ometer was their attempt at taking a scientific approach to that horrible word.

"We're going to need someone to eat lunch with," Clara said.

"Of course. Also, it would be nice if the person knew how to skateboard," Flora said.

"Or was at least interested in learning."

This led them to question #3: "Can you skateboard?" With a one-point default for a willingness to try.

"I mean, we're not great skaters," Clara said.

"Yeah, but we look good trying," Flora said. "Points for style, kid. Points for style."

Question #4 was: "Do you like to swap lunch items?" This question was meant to determine if the potential new friend was stingy and mean like Maylin. Years before, Clara and Flora had sealed their best friendship when Clara had a box of chocolate milk and Flora had just plain milk. Clara saw how Flora was eyeing her chocolate milk, she had offered to swap. "I drink chocolate milk all the time," Clara said. Which was true. But it was also true that Clara loved chocolate milk more than just about anything in the world. But Clara was like that. Just because she loved something didn't mean she wouldn't share it with you. Just thinking about it made Flora want to cry. But she was trying not to do that.

Clara said, "The last question should be a trick question. That way we know the person isn't just kissing up to us."

Flora raised an eyebrow. "Does *anyone* kiss up to us?"

Clara said, "Well, they don't. But they should, because we're awesome."

Flora nodded, "Agreed on the awesome."

Clara took the keyboard and quickly typed out question #5:

QUESTION #5: "WHAT DO YOU VALUE MOST IN A FRIEND?"

   A. Honesty

   B. Loyalty

   C. A sense of adventure

   D. No, there is no "All of the above"

Flora was confused. "That's not a trick question, Clara. The answer is C, obvs."

Clara made a bell sound—"Ding, ding, ding." She was very good at bell sounds and bird calls and other things that sounded exactly like the thing she was imitating. She said, "But a lot of people would say honesty."

Flora said, "Honesty. Schmonesty. That's such a goody two-shoes answer. Where's the fun in that?"

Clara smiled. "You're right, who needs honesty when you could be funny instead."

"But what about loyalty?" Flora asked. "Don't you want your friends to be loyal?"

Clara blew a bubble and popped it. "Pets need to be loyal. People should care about having fun."

CHAPTER 9

Día de los Tres Reyes

The Saturday before Clara moved away, their lives were made miserable by one last Saturday Spanish school event. It was January 6 and their Spanish teacher, Señorita María José, had organized a concert for Día de los Tres Reyes Magos.

As Flora pulled on her white turtleneck and navy skirt, she gave a hateful glance to the navy tights her mother had laid out for her. She wondered, *Who invented tights and what terrible vendetta was the torture device meant to settle?*

She walked down the wooden staircase in her house carefully, as the tights weren't only wildly uncomfortable, they were slippery too.

"You look very nice," her mother said approvingly.

"Thanks?" Flora said, half-heartedly. She didn't feel

very nice. She felt like ripping her tights off and putting on her favorite T-shirt, the one with all the holes and tears that her mother kept threatening to throw away. She wanted to hide under the covers until the nightmare was over and she could open her eyes and learn it had all been a bad dream: Clara and her family were not moving anywhere at all.

But in this terrible reality, they were moving. And Clara would be at the concert. She needed to spend every single moment she possibly could with her friend, even if it meant dressing in itchy clothes and singing carols in Spanish.

"¿Sonrisa?" her mother asked.

Flora made the sides of her mouth turn up, ever so slightly, but she didn't mean it and her mother knew it.

"You'll cheer up when you see Clara," her mother said. "Vámonos."

In the hallway, Flora sat on the floor and tied her boots on. She was wearing her fancy boots—the ones with the woolly lining and the polished black leather on the outside.

Her father joined them. He was dressed up too—in a fancy camel-colored coat he only wore on special occasions and sharply pleated dark slacks. Her mother wore a turtleneck dress and put on a silver parka.

Maylin stomped from her room to the top of the stairwell and said, "Do I *really* have to walk through the icy snow for this tontería?"

"It's Tres Reyes," her mother said sternly. "We are going to your sister's concert as a family."

Maylin looked unconvinced. "But I have to practice the choreography for my quince."

"Which is four months away," her mother responded.

"Believe me," Flora muttered, "she needs all the practice she can get."

Maylin liked to complain that her damas and chambelanes weren't showing up for dance rehearsal, but from what Flora had seen of Maylin flailing around the living room, her sister was far from mastering the choreography in the videos she studied with rapt attention.

"I heard that!" Maylin said.

Flora shrugged. "I was just trying to help."

"Get dressed, Maylin," her father said.

It was then that Flora noticed that her sister was still in her pajamas and the concert was starting in half an hour. "I'll be late if we wait for her," Flora said. "Just let her stay home."

"No," her mother said. "I'll take you, and your dad will wait for Maylin."

"Okay, nos vemos," Flora said, kissing her dad on the cheek. Then over her shoulder, she crossed her eyes at her sister, knowing Maylin hated it.

"You're a child," Maylin sighed.

"The favorite child," Flora countered. "See you when I see you."

As she walked out the door, Flora felt good for getting the last word in with her big sister. By her count, it was Flora-2, Maylin-0.

The day wasn't off to such a rotten start after all.

The concert was being held at the Westerly Chapel, a tiny little church not far from where Flora and her family lived. When Flora and her mother arrived, they found Clara and Mariana waiting outside.

"Oh no, I hope you haven't been waiting long," her mother said.

"Dos minutos," Mariana said cheerfully, kissing both Flora and her mother on the cheek. "Shall we find a seat?"

The mothers went left into the audience while Clara and Flora rushed backstage.

"I like your outfit," Clara joked. She was dressed identically to Flora in the school uniform: a white turtleneck, a navy skirt, and navy tights.

Flora smiled. "Twinsies."

Backstage, Señorita María José tried to get the students to quiet down. This was not easy, as all of the Spanish Saturday classes had gathered together, from the kindergartners to the eighth-grade students.

Flora and Clara took admiring surreptitious glances at a trio of eighth-grade girls wearing the same white shirts and navy miniskirts. They were only three years older, but they seemed to be infinitely cooler.

"Do you think we'll ever be that tall?" Clara whispered.

"They're tall *and* they're wearing high heels," Flora noted.

One of the girls wore her hair in two braided buns. The other two girls seemed to have fresh blow-outs and their hair fell in perfect wavy cascades, which miraculously had not gotten wet, and fallen flat, on the way to the show.

"What do you think we'll do when we get older, braids or blow-outs?" Flora asked.

"Braids for sure," Clara said. "I don't have time for fancy hairstyles."

On stage, Srta. María José placed Flora and Clara in the same row of bleachers as the eighth-grade girls. "Todos mis altos, juntos," the teacher said.

It may have been as simple as the fact that they were altos and not sopranos, but the proximity to the older students made the two girls stand a little taller and sing with more confidence.

The students sang "Los peces en el río" and the Spanish version of "Silent Night."

Srta. María José explained to the packed chapel, "'Silent Night' was originally written in German. What I try to teach my students is that while English may be the dominant language in the US, there are examples of translation, and the mixing of cultures, happening all the time. It's all around us."

To end the concert, they sang a song that Flora's mother played on repeat from the day after Thanksgiving to January sixth, when the whole family insisted she stop: "Abriendo puertas." Her mother played it so often, it was the one song from the concert that Flora didn't have to memorize—she already knew all of the words.

When they got to the chorus, the part about opening doors and closing old wounds, Clara took Flora's hand and began to salsa in place.

Flora danced alongside her and then the eighth graders noticed them and started dancing. Srta. María José gave Flora and Clara a wink, then she turned to the audience and said, "¡Bailen con nosotros! ¡Canten con nosotros!"

The audience, which consisted almost entirely of Westerly residents of Latin heritage, didn't need much prodding to take to their feet.

Flora could see their mothers in the second row, dancing with enthusiasm and beaming. To the side,

she could see her uncles bouncing baby Fina in their arms and singing along. In the back of the chapel, she saw her father swaying side to side. Sitting near the middle, she could see Abuela, her head resting on Mr. Carter's shoulder. Maylin was not dancing. She was sitting down and texting on her phone. Her Spanish was so good, she never knew the misery of having to take Saturday language classes. But instead of helping Flora, she criticized her or ignored her. Flora wondered if Maylin had never heard the saying "To whom much is given, much is expected." Maylin got to be the oldest, and the best at Spanish, and the first to have a quince. The least she could do was not ruin the holidays with her bah humbug spirit.

Srta. María José signaled them to keep singing, so they took the whole song from the top. In moments like this, Flora felt so tingly, it was like all of the night's stars had slipped down the sleeves of her shirt. Dancing and singing with her best friend, Flora thought this was what the holidays were all about, *this* is what it meant to keep abriendo puertas and viviendo la vida.

CHAPTER 10

The Long Goodbye

How do you spend your very last sleepover with your very best friend?

The answer, Flora thought, was simple—you don't sleep.

The night before Clara's family was set to move away forever, Flora dropped her overnight bag in Clara's room. "Are you good with the plan?" she asked.

Clara looked dubious. "But Flora, have you ever stayed up all night before?"

She thought about it. "The latest I've ever done is midnight on New Year's."

"Me too," Clara said. "And we usually zonk out five minutes after midnight."

Flora knew that her friend was right, but she was also feeling rather fearless. "That," she said, "is why I've made a schedule."

Clara looked intimidated. "That's quite a schedule, but I'm game to try it if you are. Let's change into our suits."

Flora felt like she was walking through her uncle's quarry warehouse as they flip-flopped from Clara's room to the pool. Nothing about Clara's house felt familiar. There was no artwork on the walls, everything was in boxes, except for the sofa, the TV, and the dining room table and chairs. It didn't feel like Clara's house and just the idea that very soon it wouldn't be Clara's house anymore made her want to cry.

The water in the pool felt cooler than usual. Even in the middle of the winter, it usually felt warm like bathwater, but tonight was different.

Flora didn't want to complain, so she swam faster, trying to warm up. But then she noticed that Clara's teeth were chattering.

"I'm cold," Clara said.

Flora looked at the clock on the wall, "But it's only six thirty. We'll never make it if we don't stick to our schedule."

"We can take extra-long showers and blast music in

the bathroom. A little post-shower dance party will take up some time."

"Okay," Flora said, climbing out of the pool. It was only when Clara handed her a fluffy robe that she realized just how cold she'd been.

Flora woke up, several hours later, on the couch. She and Clara hadn't even made it all the way through the first movie. She didn't know what time it was, but Clara's parents had turned the TV off and covered them with blankets. Clara was asleep, her knees bent, on the short side of the L-shaped couch, leaving Flora the long side. Flora considered waking Clara up and seeing if they could get back to the plan, but she didn't. The house was so dark and even if all they did was sleep, at least they were still together.

The next morning, Flora's dad took them into town for a fancy breakfast of lemon ricotta pancakes with blueberry syrup while the movers finished packing. The idea was that Clara would ride with Flora and her parents to the airport and they'd meet Clara's parents there.

After eating what may have been the largest pancakes in the whole northeast United States and most of the national blueberry syrup strategic reserves, the girls headed to the car for the final trip to the airport. The minute Clara got in the car, Flora started to cry.

Clara said, "Don't do that. You'll get me started."

It was an hour and twenty-five minutes to the airport in Connecticut. It was a long way. But neither girl felt it was long enough.

About thirty minutes into the ride, Clara said, "What if we cry so much that the car becomes submerged like a submarine?"

Flora examined the inside of her family's car as if it was something she had never seen before. "That would be a lot of tears, Clara."

"I know," Clara said, looking excited. "But wouldn't it be cool?"

Flora looked out of the window and imagined the lanes of the highway filling with water and each car turned, magically, into a submarine.

"Hmm," Flora wondered aloud. "Do you think there's traffic under the sea?"

Clara looked out the window as if she too could see all the car submarines. "I hope not," she said. "Submarine traffic would be so cotidiano."

Flora smiled. *Cotidiano* was another one of their favorite words. It was one of those words that had no exact translation to English. It meant everyday. But it also meant *like clockwork, regular schmegular,* and *right as rain.*

She looked at her best friend and said, "This day is anything but cotidiano."

"That it is not, Flora."

"Are you scared?" Flora whispered, so her parents, who were sitting in the front seat and listening to a podcast, couldn't hear.

Clara nodded. Flora noted that her friend didn't make a funny face or use a silly voice or wave her arms about dramatically. The straight answer to a serious question was so decidedly un-Clara that Flora knew that things were as bad—possibly worse—than they seemed.

"Look on the bright side," Flora said, trying to be cheerful. "Because California schools start earlier, you'll be out of school early. You'll start your new school and then in six teeny-tiny weeks, it'll be summer vacation."

Clara looked excited. "I almost forgot. I'll have almost three whole months of summer vacation."

Flora squeezed Clara's hand. "You deserve it."

Before they knew it, they were pulling into the airport.

"It can't be," Clara said incredulously, looking at all of the terminals, all of the planes going in every direction, all over the world.

Flora blinked her eyes furiously, willing herself not to start crying again.

When they pulled up to the terminal, Clara's mother was waiting for her on the curb.

"Okay, Clarita," she said when they got out of the car. "The time has come."

Clara pretended to be standing on a balcony and looked out into the distance, as if the long-term parking lot were her long-lost love. "Oh," she declared, quoting Shakespeare, "parting is such sweet sorrow."

"You're a goofball," Flora said, pulling her friend into a hug.

Clara hugged her back. "I like you goofball-y."

Flora handed Clara the map that she'd wrapped in gold paper and a set of letters. "One's for the plane. One's for when you get to your new house. One's for the first day of school."

Clara held Flora's hand. "You're not just my best friend. You are the best friend a girl could ever have."

"Same, same," Flora said.

They went back and forth, trading compliments and praises, until the airport security guard told them they had to move their car.

The girls hugged one last time. Then the moms hugged and the dads did the awkward half hug, half handshake. Then Clara went off through the door, and Flora stood there watching. She was no longer feeling so fresca. With Clara headed to California it was more like Flora la Sola now.

CHAPTER 11

Lunch Is the Loneliest Hour

In all the time that they'd been preparing for Clara's departure, Flora hadn't thought about just how awful school would be without Clara. Sitting in class, she felt like a rag doll. Like her head was full of cotton and she could barely move her arms and legs. She could hear her teacher talking; she could see the kids in the class making jokes and laughing. But she felt very far away from them and all she could hear was the big whooshing sound of air that was blowing through the hole in her heart.

When the lunch bell rang, she sat, staring into the empty space above the blackboard. The classroom emptied within seconds. She wondered if her teacher might allow her to just sit there. She didn't want to go to the cafeteria without Clara.

Her teacher, Mrs. Romano, came over and tapped her on the shoulder. "Flora, it's lunchtime."

Flora looked up and said, "I'm not hungry."

Mrs. Romano said, "I know you're sad. Today, I kept looking at Clara's chair, expecting to see her making some sort of silly face. But she's off on a new adventure and who knows, maybe this year, you'll discover an adventure of your own."

"In Westerly?" Flora asked doubtfully. The chances of her finding adventure in their small town, without Clara, were a million to one.

Mrs. Romano winked at her. "Even in Westerly. You do know this was a haven for pirates in the eighteenth century, right?"

Flora liked Mrs. Romano a lot. Social studies was one of her favorite subjects. Mrs. Romano made it fun and they studied everything from maps and geography to newspapers and documentaries that brought people from history to life.

"You've got to eat something, Flora," Mrs. Romano said. "Let me walk you to the cafeteria."

Flora willed her rag doll legs to stand and limply followed her teacher down the hall.

The day before they moved, Clara's mother brought over five trays of empanadas to Flora's parents. "Un regalito for our forever vecinos. For your freezer," she had said. There must have been more than 100 mini empanadas on those trays.

Her father had packed a special lunch for her that day: one spinach empanada, one beef, that he'd fried that very morning, then wrapped in foil. Flora knew there was also a Ramune (a Japanese soft drink), an apple, and chocolate-covered Pocky sticks. When she thought of the meal, Flora's stomach growled.

Mrs. Romano smiled and said, "See, I thought you might be hungry."

She stood with Flora at the cafeteria door and said, "Are you good?"

Flora nodded, but she looked out at the room and thought, *I am anything but good.*

The cafeteria was loud and raucous, and the two teachers assigned to keep order sat at opposite ends of the cafeteria, nibbling mindlessly at sandwiches and scrolling through their phones.

It was a small school, just two classes for every grade. Flora knew everyone, but looking around the room, she felt close to no one.

There was the table of Lucys. That was out. The Lucys were the popular girls in the class. A girl named Palmer Gilroy and her cronies, Sasha C. and Sasha M. Clara and Flora started calling them Lucy in the fourth grade because they were like the girl in Peanuts who was always moving the football just when Charlie Brown was about to kick it. (Needless to say, Maylin was a total Lucy.)

The Lucys were always changing their mind about what was cool or not. One week, cheesy fries were "ah-mazing." And poké would be declared "the worst." Two weeks later, it was just the exact opposite. They were all making plans to go to the poké place after school and wondering aloud: "Whatever compelled us to put even one cheesy fry in our mouths??!"

Flora wondered if they were really flesh and blood girls at all. Maybe, she thought, they were robots, programmed to run experiments on the susceptible nature of the pre-adolescent mind.

She saw Daisy and Olivia, two math geniuses who were so smart, they took an advanced math class at the high school two days a week. They were nice, but

Flora could never understand what they were talking about. In class one day, Daisy had made a joke about bell curves and something about Bayes leaf probabilities and their math teacher, Ms. Padnani, had laughed so hard that they thought snot might come out of her nose. It was like Daisy and Olivia spoke their own language. Flora had enough of a tough time keeping up with Spanish. She didn't want to add geometry and all of its clever references to the list of things she was trying to learn.

A boy named Aidan called out to her, "Hey Flora, come sit with us."

The twins Aidan and Aditya had been in Flora's classes since preschool. They were very *very* fifth grade. By this, Flora meant that they did one dance again and again, a move they'd culled from their favorite video game, until some grown-up begged them to stop. They thought anything that involved farts and burps were hilarious. But what Aidan and Aditya loved more than anything was food. They spent all their free time watching chef shows and challenging each other to eat insane amounts of food.

They were always having competitions. Who could eat the most Peeps? Who could eat three mini apple pies in under ten minutes? Who could eat the most French fries and bowls of ice cream without throwing up?

To time these competitions, they both wore identical stopwatches on cords around their necks. Just like their gym teacher, Ms. Behar.

Aidan and Aditya's mother was a doctor at the same hospital as Flora's mother. They were kind of like little brothers, even though they were all in the same grade. Flora figured there were worse places to eat lunch. She walked over to their table, trying to erase the sadness from her face.

"What's up?" she said, trying to smile.

"Not much," Aditya said.

"So Clara moved, huh?" Aidan said.

Flora nodded.

"Where'd she go?"

"California."

"North or South?"

Flora wondered why he even cared.

"Northern California," she said.

Aidan opened his laptop and pulled up a spreadsheet on his computer.

"There's some good challenges up there. At the Monrovia Cheese Steak Emporium, there's a contest where you have to eat eight classic cheesesteaks and eight sides of fries in two hours."

Flora shrugged. "Would that be hard?"

Aidan and Aditya exchanged glances.

"Um, do you know how *big* those sandwiches are?" Aidan asked.

Aditya held his arms to the length of his laptop. "They're like THIS BIG."

Aidan shook his head. "Bigger than that."

"Okay," Flora said. "What's the prize?"

"You get a hundred-dollar gift card and your picture on the Wall of Fame," Aidan said.

"That's so cool," Aditya said, high-fiving Aidan as if they'd just won the contest.

Flora thought about it for a second. "I think if I ate that many cheesesteaks in a single sitting, I'd never want to eat another cheesesteak for a very long time. So the gift card wouldn't be that great."

Aidan and Aditya looked at her as if she'd said something unspeakable.

"The prize is cool," Aditya said. "You could give the gift card to a friend."

"Like me," Aidan said.

"And anyway, it's not really about the prize," Aditya explained. "It's about the glory."

"Yeah," Aidan chimed in. "The. Wall. Of. Fame." He said the four words as if he was the guy in the movie theater who tells you to silence your cell phones and not to talk during the film.

Aidan tabbed through his spreadsheet. "There's a ton of good contests near Clara. Ice cream. Cupcakes. Pizza. Moon pies."

Flora nodded, not wanting to hurt their feelings.

Aidan smiled. "I could email this list to you and you could share them with Clara."

"Cool, thanks," Flora said.

Aidan hit send and said, "Done."

"Tell her to make a video if she actually enters any of the contests," Aditya said. "We want to see her."

"Okay," Flora said, thinking never ever would she or Clara do such a thing.

Then it occurred to her that since Clara was gone, to the very opposite end of the country, the truth was she couldn't say with certainty what Clara might or might not do in her new life.

"Flora," Aidan said, "did you hear that a man in California downed three scotch bonnet peppers in eight and half seconds?"

Flora shrugged. "I had no idea."

Aditya said, "That's a huge deal, Flora. It's in the Guinness Book of World Records!" Flora didn't know what that was, but she thought it best not to interrupt them.

"One day I'm going to beat that record," Aidan said.

"Not if I beat the record first," Aditya said.

Flora was pretty sure that no matter what might change, her best friend would not have scotch bonnet peppers as a life goal. Surely, the boys must have something else they could talk about.

Flora looked at her watch as she polished off the last bite of her very delicious empanada. She thought her watch must be broken. When she and Clara had lunch together, the lunch period always seemed so so short.

How could it be that there was still twenty minutes left before she could go back to class?

"Hey Flora," Aidan said.

"Hey Aidan," she answered.

"Did you know there's a contest in New Mexico where people compete to see who can eat the most garlic cloves in a single sitting?"

"I know now," Flora said wanly.

Aditya started giggling. "It's called the 'You Stink' contest."

Aidan guffawed, exposing a very unseemly half-eaten hunk of chocolate cake. "'You Stink'! That's the best contest name ever."

Flora looked at her watch again. Eighteen minutes until lunch was over. As her grandmother would say, "you get what you get and you don't get upset." This was her lunch table now. She had to just deal with it. No use getting upset.

CHAPTER 12

Zoom Fail

Sunday evening was Flora's new favorite time of the week. After dinner her time and lunch Clara's time, she and Clara met up for a chat on Zoom.

Flora loved everything about the calls. The fun started when she poured herself a glass of chocolate milk, knowing that Clara would be pouring herself the same thing.

Flora made the call from her room and she always hopped on early to change her background. Sometimes she made it into a Disney castle. Once, she made it the surface of the moon.

That day, Flora chose to situate herself in the Batcave under a giant Wanted poster of the Joker. She smiled, knowing that it would make Clara laugh.

For five minutes, she was alone in the call. She

stared at herself and tried, in vain, to tame the curly pouf of her hair that always seemed like it was determined to secede from the nation of curls on her head.

After ten minutes, she started to get worried—but she knew Clara was sometimes late. She sent Clara a text saying "Hey."

By the time she'd been alone on the call for fifteen minutes, she was pretty sure something was horribly wrong.

She bounded down the stairs and found her father in the den. He was watching the detective show that had eight thousand episodes. She entered the room, just as the detectives arrived at the crime scene.

"Argh," she said. She grabbed the remote and turned the screen off.

"¿Qué pasa?" her father asked, sounding more than a little annoyed.

"Something's wrong with Clara," Flora said. "Can you call her parents? I waited fifteen minutes on the call and she never showed up. She's not answering my texts."

Flora found her mind rushing with thoughts of all the terrible things that could happen to Clara in that strange and terrible land that was California. "She could have gone to the beach and been attacked by a shark."

The thought was crazy, but once the tears started, she couldn't make them stop.

"Ay, niña, cálmate," her father said, wrapping her in his arms. "Don't let your very vivid imagination run away with you."

"But there must be something awfully wrong for her to miss our call."

Maylin walked into the living room and looked at Flora crying. "Who died?" she asked, before looking at her smartphone to read about someone somewhere else who was definitely not dealing with the terrible disappearance of her best friend.

Flora couldn't believe it. Her very best friend in the world could be lying on a beach, limbless from a shark attack, and Maylin was just being her usual—a quién le importa—self.

"Nobody died," her father said. "Flora, wait here. I'm going to step outside and call Clara's father." Maylin shrugged and left the room.

Flora sat on the sofa, her left knee wiggling wildly, the way it did when she was nervous. She put both of her hands on her knee and willed it to stop moving. Her father stepped back into the living room and the smile on his face made Flora instantly relax.

"Clara is okay," he said. "She has a new friend named Avery, who invited her to go on a hike in the Redwoods."

Flora couldn't quite believe what she was hearing. What friend? "But she never misses our call."

"She left early this morning, maybe she thought she'd be back on time."

"But she didn't even text me."

Her father shook his head. "Apparently, she forgot her phone at home. Her parents aren't too happy about that."

Flora wasn't satisfied. "She knows my number by heart. She could have borrowed a phone and texted me."

"Querida," her father sighed. "She probably just forgot."

The word echoed in Flora's head like a hammer: Forgot. Forgot. Forgot.

Clara had been gone for all of three months and she'd already forgotten her.

"Okay, Papá," Flora said, trying to sound brave. "I'll be in my room."

Flora climbed the stairs slowly and slumped in front of the seat at her desk. The Batman cave background was still on her screen. But now it seemed like the Joker was laughing *at* her.

She heard a knock on her door and fought the urge to call out *go away*. She knew her parents would tell her not to be rude. So she quietly said, "Come in."

It wasn't her mother. Or her father. It was Maylin. Flora wished she'd just taken the chance and told her to get lost.

Maylin said, "Hey, look. I know you're bummed that Clara missed your call. I get it. Qué mala onda."

Flora stared at the laptop. She couldn't start crying again. Not because she didn't want to but because she was 99.9 percent sure she had no tears left.

Maylin said, "I have some free time. How about I wash your hair and French braid it?"

Flora didn't know what to say. Maylin hadn't volunteered to spend time with her in, like, forever.

"Okay," Flora said tentatively.

Maylin treated Flora like she was a customer in the fanciest salon.

She turned on the wireless speaker in the bathroom that they shared and sang along to the Latin trap tracks that pulsated through the room.

Maylin washed and conditioned Flora's hair, giving her scalp a gentle massage as she washed the products in and out. Then she brushed through Flora's hair, applying hair serums and other products that she would normally *never* let Flora touch, much less use.

Then Maylin put a face mask on Flora.

"Qué raro," Flora said, touching the cold, slightly slimy paper that was stuck on her face.

"Look at you," Maylin said. "Breaking out the Spanish."

When Maylin had finished braiding her hair, Flora felt herself getting teary again—but in a good way. Her mother was always saying "Sisters take care of each other."

Maybe it was actually true.

"Gracias, hermana," Flora said.

"No hay problema," Maylin said. "I have to do twenty

hours of charity for my Rotary Club scholarship. Counseling the forlorn and hopelessly incompetent wasn't on the list of suggested activities, but I'll make it work."

She winked at Flora.

Maylin stood then and just as she was about to leave Flora's room, she said, "De veras, chica. You and Clara go back like car seats. If she misses a Zoom every once in a while, give her a break. Nobody's perfect. Not her. Not you. Nadie."

For the first time, in a long time, Flora was grateful to have Maylin around.

CHAPTER 13

Replaced

It had only taken Clara three weeks to meet a girl who she says scored 3 out of 5 on the BFF-ometer. Her name was Avery and she couldn't skate, and she didn't speak another language. But she wanted to study Arabic someday. Most importantly, Avery's dad was a chef and he made what looked like *the* most incredible grilled cheese sandwiches. Flora pulled up her BFF-ometer. Avery didn't seem like much of a 3 to her.

Flora's parents wouldn't let her have Instagram, but Clara had an account, and a full 50 percent of her feed now consisted of photos of fancy grilled cheese sandwiches: scrumptious, gooey cheddar served with a side of marinara, for dipping. Grilled mascarpone cheese, chocolate sauce, and sliced bananas. There was even a sandwich with mac and cheese inside, which was only surpassed in likes by a sandwich with mac and cheese *and* short rib inside. There were days when Flora wondered what she envied more: Clara's new friendship or the food that came along with it.

Flora tried not to act jealous on calls with Clara.

"So how's Avery?" she asked, feigning friendliness.

"She's great!" Clara said, clearly pretending not to notice Flora's fake tone. "It's fun to have a friend whose dad is a chef."

"I bet," Flora mumbled.

"Ay Flora, no seas así," Clara said. "You should be happy for me."

"I am!" Flora said, smiling tightly.

"I know you, Flora," Clara said. "You're still my best friend. Avery's my California friend, that's all. So how's it going, Flora? Any contenders?"

Flora told her that there weren't. Just lunch with Aidan and Aditya and an inordinate and vexing amount of talk about scotch bonnet peppers.

Flora liked using fancy words like *inordinate* and

vexing. She had fantasies of being in a spelling bee and winning a giant prize by correctly spelling all of the words she used to describe Maylin. She imagined that afterwards when the local television news station interviewed her and asked how she'd acquired a vocabulary that was both so sophisticated and withering, words that certainly didn't come up in most fifth-grade lesson plans, she would just smile and say, "Have you met my sister?"

Clara jumped to her overly optimistic persona and said, "Hey, not so fast. Maybe we're overlooking the obvious. The BFF-ometer wasn't programmed to ask questions about gender. Maybe the boys could be your placeholder pals."

Flora shrugged. She didn't think so. Aidan and Aditya were okay—for lunch. But she couldn't imagine inviting them over after school or confiding in them about how Maylin tormented her.

"Hey Flora, maybe you're not giving them a chance," Clara said.

Flora said, "Hmm. You think? Aidan actually slept through STEM class when Mrs. Fessimier was teaching us JavaScript with this cool program called Code Monster. And Aditya rides his skateboard like a toddler on a sled."

Clara was tearing through a pack of strawberry Twizzlers on their call. She'd always been a girl who liked her snacks. Clara chewed, then said, "Hey, maybe he was tired."

Flora shook her head. "No, I *asked* him if he was tired and he said he was bored. Bored during STEM? I mean, in what universe?"

Clara said, "I like Aidan, but you have a point. Don't give up, Flora. And guess what, I have some good news!"

Flora smirked and said, "You're moving back to Rhode Island?"

Clara said, "Not-*that*-good good news. But my mom said that she might let me come back to Rhode Island and go to sleepaway camp with you."

Flora felt like her heart was floating like a balloon and for a second she thought her whole body might lift, ever so slightly, off the ground.

"Camp Hoover?" she asked.

She had never been to sleepaway camp, but she had spent a good amount of her considerable free time looking at camps online. If she and Clara could go to sleepaway camp together, life would be good again—at least for a little while.

Clara said, "I don't know which one. But my mom is talking to your mom."

"That is very good news," Flora said. She did some quick math in her head. Summer vacation was only sixty-three days and roughly twelve hours away. She didn't need the BFF-ometer. Clara would be back soon enough.

CHAPTER 14

Dance Class

When Clara moved, Flora's parents decided they didn't want her walking home from school by herself. So each day after school, Flora went to her father's shop instead. She didn't mind.

She was so proud of her father's store. It was only two years old and it was a giant leap from the years he spent making and selling furniture from their basement.

Flora always paused at the front door and smiled when she saw the sign that said:

HECHO A MANO:
CONTEMPORARY FURNITURE DESIGN

The store was a big open space with dining tables, desks, bookcases—all made by her father. There was a side table made of multiple wood blocks that looked like the fanciest checkerboard you'd ever seen. Her father sold lots of his famous boombox bookcases—they were a pair of curved wooden bookcases, in the most beautiful butter-colored oak. And when you put the two cases together, they looked like speakers.

But Flora's favorite piece in the entire store was a coffee table shaped like a surfboard. Flora always had to fight the temptation to jump on it. She knew if she ever did, she'd be in a heap of trouble. And yet . . . the thought came to her every time she visited the store: How much fun it would be to hop onto the wooden surfboard structure and pretend she was riding the waves.

She kissed her father on the cheek and set her bookbag on the desk next to his.

"Hola, Flora!" he said. "How was school?"

"Good," she said. But she meant tolerable. Which is what life was like now that Clara had moved away. She wondered if she should go to the library and try to find more information about the pirates of Westerly, the ones Mrs. Romano had mentioned. Or maybe just make up the stories on her own with neighbors starring as looters and thieves with peg legs and swords. She hadn't had any fun in what felt like a very long time.

"Well, your mother has to work late tonight, she's got an important surgery. So we're going to go with Maylin to her dance rehearsal."

Maylin had been about 2.5 percent nicer since the time Clara had missed the Zoom call with Flora, but she still was a total and complete quincezilla.

"Noooo," Flora called out. "Can't I just stay home by myself?"

Her father shook his head.

"Her rehearsal is only an hour. And the choreographer said you can stand in the back and learn the moves. It'll be good for you to get out of the house."

"I get out of the house," Flora said. "I go to school. I come here. I go to Spanish school."

"Afterwards, we'll get pizza," her father said. "You can pick the toppings and Maylin can't complain."

The dance rehearsal was in a room of the Westerly Rec Center that Flora had never seen. The walls were painted black. One wall was covered with floor-to-ceiling mirrors. The other wall had a wooden rod across it that Flora recognized as a ballet barre. She and Clara had taken exactly *one* ballet class in the second grade and then declared their mutual hate for tights, tutus, and everything pink, so their mothers said they didn't have to return.

But this room was really different. The floor was a beautiful chocolate-colored wood and the lighting fixtures were round like wagon wheels. The word that came to Flora's mind was *glamorous*. Like the Audrey Hepburn movies her mother liked to watch. On the wall opposite the mirrors was a neon sign that said "Dance your ♥ out."

Flora liked everything about this dance studio. She couldn't wait to tell Clara all about it. It was so much cooler than the place where they'd taken ballet. That place looked like a unicorn had vomited sparkles and confetti all over it.

The choreographer, Nina, was a cool college student in a cropped tank, oversized sweatpants, and sneakers.

Maylin stood between two Panamanian teenage

boys that Flora recognized from parties at her uncles' house. On her right were Maylin's two best friends, who she was surprised to see were not staring at their phones for the very first time in their lives.

Flora thought Maylin looked nervous.

She said, "I can't believe people keep missing rehearsal. I want this dance to be good, like viral-video good."

Nina, the choreographer, said, "It's all good, Maylin. Is that your sister joining us tonight?"

Maylin turned to glance at Flora. "Stay in the back and stay out of my way," she said in a kind of whisper but really designed for everyone to hear.

The choreographer walked over to Flora and said, "Hey, welcome to the party. Just do what you can."

Then she turned on the music, a booming reggae-ton beat. She stood in front of the mirrored wall and addressed the group. She said, "Let's get started. And remember, we're here for a good time, not a long time. Just have fun with it."

Flora watched carefully as Nina broke down each move: "Step left, right, left and switch. Step right, left, right and switch."

It surprised her how easily the moves came to her. Whenever she and Clara saw dances on TikTok, she assumed that they were just making it up as they went along. But Nina showed her that it was all about breaking it down into little steps. Nina said, "First the legs. Then you add the arms. Then we flow it all together."

Flora kept dancing, proud of how well she could follow the instructions.

"Maylin," Nina said, pointing. "Your little sister's pretty good. Are you *sure* you don't want her to dance with you at your quince?"

Maylin didn't even turn to look at Flora. She said, "She's ten. I'm not going to have an elementary school kid dancing at my quince."

Nina shrugged. "It's your party, Mamita."

Flora didn't care. It was just a treat to be in that cool room, learning all of those steps. She felt like she was more than dancing. She felt like she was flying.

After class, Flora, Maylin, and their dad picked up a pizza: half olive, since that was their mom's favorite, and half salami, Flora's favorite. Maylin complained, but her dad wasn't having it.

Flora had really liked going to Maylin's class. She'd been so busy learning the choreography, she hadn't thought about how much she missed Clara. "Maylin, I really liked your dance class. Would it be okay if I came along on Wednesday nights?"

"Fine," Maylin sighed. "But stay in the back. Vista pero no escuchada."

Maylin's dad smiled. "I love it. Mis hijas doing something together for once."

Later that night, as she brushed her teeth, Flora could hear Maylin on the phone. "Sí, Frankie. She'll be coming to class on Wednesdays. You see the way she looks at me. She idolizes me. What can I say? I'm her hero."

Flora nearly sputtered a mouthful of toothpaste all over the bathroom sink. It was the funniest thing she had heard. Maybe ever. She couldn't wait until her next call with Clara to tell her what Maylin said. This was too juicy for a text. Maylin? Her hero? It was so funny, Flora very nearly laughed herself to sleep.

CHAPTER 15

Cállate, Niña

The following Monday, Flora's parents let her and Maylin stay up to watch the presidential debates. As the candidates gathered on the stage, Flora asked her father questions about who they were and the issues they would be speaking about in the debate.

Maylin spent the entire time looking at her phone, trying on hairstyles with some stupid app. It would have been one thing if she sat quietly at the other end of the sectional, snapping selfies and uploading them.

But she kept talking nonstop—out loud—to no one in particular. "The thing is . . ." Maylin said, talking over the candidates.

Flora said, "Come on, Maylin, I'm trying to listen." But Maylin ignored her.

Maylin went on, "I always pictured myself with bangs and a bob for my quince. But I feel like twenty years from now when I look back on these pictures, that's a choice I could regret. I may just be asking myself, *Maylin, chica, what part of classic updo did you not understand?*"

Maylin seemed to think her fifteenth birthday was a national holiday, but Flora knew that a lot of important things were happening in the world.

Flora threw a pillow at her. "Can you please keep it down? They are talking about immigration and border control, stuff that actually matters."

Maylin threw the pillow back at Flora. "This matters. Even at fifteen, you have to have an appreciation for timeless style!"

Flora rolled her eyes. "You're not even fifteen yet."

Her parents were so engrossed in the debate, they didn't seem to notice how distracting Maylin was. Flora thought, *If it was me, they would totally be all like* cállate, niña. Sometimes it seemed that Maylin's voice was like that pitch that only dogs could hear. Except in this case, Flora was the dog who was being driven loca.

"Hair extensions are another quandary altogether," Maylin squawked. "Celeb stylists swear by them. They're not expensive and they look great in photos. I just think if I'm sweating it out on the dance floor and a clip-in piece of my hair goes flying across the room, I'll be horrified. Worse, what if someone makes a video and uploads it to YouTube and it goes viral?"

"Oh. My. God. Shut up!" Flora yelled.

Both of Flora's parents turned around at that. "Flora la Fresca, no," her mother said. "No seas tan americana."

Don't be so American. As if everything that differentiated her from her big sister had to do with where they were born or how well they spoke Spanish.

Flora *wanted* to say, "I'm actually nicer than Maylin." If nicer was more Panamanian, then Flora would win.

Flora *wanted* to say, "Come on, shush her, not me." But it was as if Maylin had cast a spell over them and they couldn't hear her incessant chattering. Flora had long thought Maylin was part bruja, or part witch. But never had the evidence been more undeniable.

Maylin, still talking over presidential candidates, said, "I've always wanted to have a viral video. Pero tú sabes, you want your video to be of something positive, not negative. Hmmm, what could I do to have a viral video?"

On the TV, a candidate was talking about climate change. Flora had written an essay about the topic in fourth grade and come in second place in a statewide competition.

"Come on, Maylin, just let me hear what she has to say."

Maylin didn't answer Flora directly, she just nodded distractedly.

"It's imperative that we continue our stance as an international leader in climate change and drawdown," the candidate said.

Maylin, oblivious to the fact that all of the storms that had hit Rhode Island might have something to do with climate change, said, "You know, I was thinking. It could rain, which would make my backyard quince a disaster."

"What's the worst-case scenario on climate change?" the candidate continued, looking sincerely into the camera. "We don't have to use our imaginations. We're already seeing hints of it—extreme heat, rising sea levels. And the most vulnerable among us will suffer the greatest."

Maylin said into the phone, "Maybe my quince shouldn't be about me? Maybe it's about all the children who don't have money for a quince, who are suffering the most. I could have the party at a children's hospital. We could bring all the food and the music there—you know, to cheer them up. Then the viral video could be of me, dressed up in my quince dress, dancing with a really sick kid in a hospital gown. Just sharing my shine. The way I do."

Flora looked at her parents, seated together on the couch. "Do you hear this locura?"

Her mother said, "What? The candidates are making really good points."

Maylin looked at her sharply and said, "¿Tienes algo que decir?"

"Did you hear her saying she wants to have her quince at a children's hospital?"

"Very kind of you to even have thought of it, niña," her mother said.

"That's a sweet idea," Flora's dad said. "But the deposit we gave the tent company is non-refundable. We'll be doing the quince here."

Flora muttered to herself, "Forget about the idea, how about the fact that your idea is *ridonkulous* and obnoxious."

She couldn't wait to tell Clara about Maylin's idea of having her quince at a children's hospital. It was, quite possibly, the most terrible, horrible, no good, very bad example of "doing it for the 'gram."

She looked at the clock. It was ten p.m. The joy of staying up late was totally flattened by having to listen to Maylin's mindless chatter.

"It's late. I'm going to bed," Flora said.

She kissed her mother on the cheek.

"Duérmete bien, querida," her mom said.

Her father opened his arms for an embrace.

"Wasn't Maylin the worst tonight?" she whispered.

"She's a teenager and the quince is a thing. She's not so bad, chica," he said.

It couldn't just be that her parents thought Maylin was perfect and could no wrong. Maybe, just maybe, her father had been replaced by a robot. That was the only thing that made sense.

She made a note to explore further on Saturday afternoon. Inevitably, between the morning and afternoon soccer games, her father fell asleep on the couch for a good thirty-minute nap. When he was asleep, nothing could wake him. Flora would examine him for signs of robot wiring then.

CHAPTER 16

Blazers? Blazes!

It was April and Clara had been gone for four long and miserable months when a new girl arrived in Flora's class. Her name was Zaidee Khal. She had moved to their town from Paris. Flora couldn't wait to tell Clara that a bona fide French kid had showed up at their school.

The second thing Flora noticed was that she—the new girl—looked more like a grown-up than a kid. She was as tall as their teacher Mrs. Romano.

The next thing Flora noticed was that her hair had been blown out that morning. Flora knew this because once a month, Maylin got a blow-out at the mall. Zaidee Khal had those same bouncy shampoo commercial waves.

When Mrs. Romano called her to the front of the room, she looked like she was being followed by a wind machine. She was wearing jeans, a crisp white shirt, and a navy-blue blazer with little gold buttons. Flora rolled her eyes. *Who wears blazers?* she thought. *To the fifth grade?*

Then she looked at Zaidee Khal's shoes. She was wearing leopard-print ballet slippers. Flora couldn't believe the levels of fancy on this girl. She was willing to bet the crisp twenty-dollar bill her abuela had sent her for her birthday that it would take Zaidee Khal all of twenty-four hours to become a Lucy.

When it was time to go to lunch, Mrs. Romano asked Flora to show Zaidee to the cafeteria. Flora knew better than to groan or make a face. Instead, she did this thing she'd taught herself to do: She smiled widely, then made a low growl, like a bear ransacking a trash can for food, in the back of her throat. Only she could hear it but it made her happy, which made her smile even more. It was a pretty good trick.

As the two girls walked down the hallway, Flora tried to point out interesting things to Zaidee.

"That's the gym. Mrs. Behar is the gym teacher. She's super nice."

Zaidee just nodded, like a grown-up reading emails on their phone when you're trying to tell them a really good story. Flora thought, *This chica couldn't care less.*

Still, she was the new girl and Flora had been charged with showing her the ropes. She proudly showed her around the cafeteria: the hot lunch line, the little cafe counter that sold everything from tuna sandwiches to Japanese rice balls and the vending machine that had everything from sparkling water to sodas to electric-blue and fire engine–red drinks.

"I brought my lunch," Zaidee said, casting a disgusted eye on the vending machine.

"Cool," Flora said, trying not to feel offended.

Flora walked Zaidee into the lunchroom and deposited her at the table of Lucys. She introduced them by their real names, of course. She said, "Palmer, Sasha 1 and Sasha 2, this is Zaidee. She's new here. Be nice." Zaidee sat down, curving her freakishly long legs around what seemed like a doll-size bench in proportion to her grown-up height.

Flora was walking away when she heard Zaidee say something weird. She said, "Aren't you going to eat with us?"

Flora shook her head and pointed to a table on the far side of the room. "I'm going to sit with those two."

She had pointed to Aidan and Aditya. The boys were trying to see who could eat the most hot dogs at the fastest speed. This was, as you might imagine, not a pleasant thing to watch. But they had seen a Japanese competitive eater down fifty-eight hot dogs in ten minutes and ever since they had been obsessed with beating that record.

"Who are those guys?" Zaidee asked, seeming genuinely curious.

"You don't want to know," one of the Lucys said dismissively.

Zaidee looked at the two boys, their cheeks looking painfully stuffed with hot dog meat, and said, in a super slow voice, "Okaaaaay."

As Flora walked away, she felt a little bad. Did Blazer Girl actually want to be friends?

* * *

Flora sat down at the table with the two boys and took out a book, along with her sandwich.

"Hey, are you going to read a book the whole time?" Aditya said, looking offended.

Flora didn't look up from her book. She just said, "Yes."

"Come on," Aditya said. "Talk to us."

Flora looked up. "It's a really good book."

If she was being perfectly honest, it was her third time reading *The Graveyard Book*, but the great thing was that every time she read it, it was a little less scary.

"Hey Flora, we know you miss Clara," Aidan said.

"But we're not chopped liver."

"How do you make chopped liver anyway?" Aidan asked.

Flora marveled at how *any* mention of food distracted him.

"I don't know. You be the chopper, I'll be the liver," Aditya said, laying his head on the table while Aidan did karate chops across his back.

"Now it's my turn," Aditya said. "I get to be the chopper."

Flora took out her phone and held it under the table. They weren't supposed to use devices during school hours, but she couldn't wait.

"Dear Clara," she typed. "I miss you so much. You have no idea."

CHAPTER 17

To Soda or Not to Soda, That Is the Question.

The next week, Mrs. Romano announced that their class, 5B, would spend the next month learning the techniques of debate. Each week she would put forth a resolution and then two students would debate the topic. The school principal would judge the merit of the arguments and the effectiveness of the debater's argument.

"The first topic will be soda vending machines in schools, an issue that has sparked a lot of interest around here in the last few weeks," Mrs. Romano began. "Flora LeFevre will lead the affirmative team."

Flora felt nervous and excited. She had been watching the presidential debates with her parents ever since she was a little kid. Her parents never missed an important debate. They watched from beginning to end, listening carefully to how the candidates discussed everything from education to climate change to foreign policy. Her parents especially disliked when candidates got snarky. They disliked when candidates were disrespectful to each other with lines like, "There you go again" or "Do you even know what you're talking about?"

Mrs. Romano then said, "I'd like the newest member of our class, Zaidee Khal, to lead the opposing team."

She went on to explain that the proceedings would begin with the affirmative team, who would have ten minutes to explain why the school should keep the soda machines.

Mrs. Romano went around the room and assigned the teams without any regard to what made sense. She put Harper on Zaidee's team along with one of the Lucys, Palmer Gilroy.

Flora looked over at Aidan, who pointed to himself, then pointed at Flora, then threw his fists up as if they were about to jump into a boxing ring.

"Flora," Mrs. Romano said, "what you and your team need to do is show us the strength of your argument."

She walked around the classroom and then she began to sing, "You've got to *accentuate the positive . . .* and *eliminate* the negative."

Flora had never heard that song before, but she was impressed. Mrs. Romano had a *really* good voice. *She should go on one of those TV singing contests, and bring us along as her special in-studio cheering team,* Flora thought.

Mrs. Romano continued. "The judge, our esteemed principal, Jen Sargent, will be looking for you to tell us why keeping the soda machines is a good thing for the school. In debate, the positive points are called advantages. Then she'll be looking for you to tell us what we stand to lose by removing the machines, those are called 'harms.'"

Flora raised her hand. "I know you're a teacher and everything, but how do you know so much about debating?"

Mrs. Romano smiled and then she looked kind of shy. "Very insightful question, Flora. I may or may not have been state debate champ in high school two years in a row . . . Okay, I'm being coy. I totally was."

The classroom buzzed. The soda machines were a

big deal and most of the kids didn't want to see them go. Moreover, it was starting to become clear that the debate activity was just a fancy way of saying "Go fight this out (with big words) and we'll give you a grade on it." Which nobody minded.

Aidan raised his hand and Mrs. Romano called on him. "If you were two-time debate club champ, then why did you become a teacher? My mom says that if you can argue well, you can make a lot of money as a lawyer."

Mrs. Romano looked like she was a little bit at a loss. Everybody knew that teachers didn't get paid anywhere near what they deserved. Flora thought, *Leave it to Aidan to try to put a price tag on it. He's sooo competitive.* She wished there was a plate of hot dogs around to distract him.

But Mrs. Romano recovered quickly. "Aidan, that is absolutely true that you can use debate in any number of professions. Our focus today and this month is how debate can help us augment our critical thinking. Now let's talk about what we'll be looking for the opposing team to do."

Flora looked at Zaidee and was immediately intimidated by her notebook, which was, even after only a few days, filled with perfect penmanship notes. Flora's own notebook had as many drawings as notes. She was currently drawing a cartoon about a ninja battle between an army of tacos and a battalion of sushi.

She thought that if she was the new girl in school, like Zaidee, she'd be nervous about leading a debate team. But Zaidee didn't seem nervous at all. Flora noticed that she sat perfectly straight in her chair. She didn't slouch or hunch over the desk like most of the kids.

Flora liked slouching. In fact, she thought if there were an Olympics for slouching, she could get a gold medal. She thought of Vinyl Sundays where she and her dad listened to records together and how some of their favorite singers like Gwen Stefani and Shirley Manson made slouching look stylish and cool.

Her team consisted of Niklas, who was obsessed with basketball and spent every second of recess and PE practicing his NBA moves. That was okay, Flora could work with that. Niklas was super focused and got good grades. Flora knew that she could count on him not to interrupt debate practice with stupid jokes or goofy fart noises. The other member of her team was Daisy, who was a quiet genius. She had a 4.7 grade point average because not only did she get A's on everything, she aced the bonus questions on every exam. Flora just hoped that Daisy, who rarely spoke above a whisper, would speak up during the actual debate.

Mrs. Romano explained that the opposing team would then present arguments that opposed the resolution. The second speakers would present affirming and opposing arguments. Then there would be a short break while each team prepared a five-minute rebuttal.

Aditya started giggling and raised his hand.

Flora knew what he was going to say before he even opened his trap.

"Yes, Aditya," Mrs. Romano said.

"The word *rebuttal* has got a big old butt in the middle of it," he said.

Most of the boys started laughing then while

everyone else waited patiently for them to calm down. When they didn't, Mrs. Romano said, "Okay, enough! Calm down. It's not even that funny."

Mrs. Romano then explained that the competition would end with closing arguments and Ms. Sargent would choose the winning team.

"What does the winning team get?" Palmer asked.

What a bunch of Lucys, Flora thought.

Ms. Sargent explained that the winning team would get gift cards to the local bookstore. And at the end of the debate cycle, when all of the students had competed, the entire class would get a pizza party to celebrate their hard work.

Aidan put his hand up.

Flora knew before he even asked that his question would be about food. He and Aditya talked about food all the time.

Aidan asked, "Will there be soda at the pizza party?"

Mrs. Romano smiled. "Depends on which side presents the winning argument."

CHAPTER 18

We're Not Friends

That day, when the school bell rang, Zaidee ran to catch up with Flora. She said, "Hey, do you want to meet to work with me on the debate project?"

Flora wondered what kind of evil ulterior plan the new girl was concocting.

"We're on opposing sides, remember?" Flora said.

"I know, but I did debate club at my old school in France and it's actually kind of fun if we all meet and go through things together, even though we will split into opposing sides."

Flora didn't get it. "Then you'll know all of my ideas and you'll come up with rebuttals to kick my butt."

Zaidee said, "It will actually help us both prepare stronger arguments if we test our ideas out before the actual debate. We can meet for lunch tomorrow and go over some videos of classic high school debates."

Flora shook her head. "We're not allowed to use devices in school . . . but I can ask Mrs. Romano if we could use an iPad and eat lunch in the classroom tomorrow."

Zaidee looked pleased. "Sounds like a plan, Stan."

Flora wanted to tell her that nobody had used that expression since second grade. But that seemed mean and unnecessary.

The next day at lunchtime, they stayed in the classroom and Flora opened the iPad, which Mrs. Romano was able to throw to a big screen that covered the blackboard.

"I'm so glad you girls are taking your roles as leaders of the first teams so seriously," Mrs. Romano said. "I'm going to step out, but I'll be back at the end of the period."

Flora took out one of her favorite lunches: leftover ropa vieja, with rice and beans.

Zaidee gave Flora's lunch a withering glance.

"What?" Flora said. "It's beef with rice and beans." Then she added, "It's a Latin dish."

"I know what ropa vieja is," Zaidee said. Her Spanish accent was, like everything about her, perfect.

Flora felt impatient, bothered.

"How are you going to eat it cold?" Zaidee looked around. "Isn't there a microwave?"

It was the first non-Lucy thing she'd said all day. Although Flora hated to agree with her, the new girl was right.

It was true that room temperature ropa vieja was not the most delicious thing in the world. But Flora had this Jedi mind trick that before she took a bite, she pictured her Sunday dinner with her whole family crowded around the dining table. She imagined what the ropa vieja smelled like, sizzling on the stove, and how good it had looked on the table, with the steam rising from it. Then she closed her eyes and took a bite. If she was very quiet and still, she could almost imagine the food was hot the whole entire time she was eating it.

Needless to say, this wasn't something Flora shared with *Mademoiselle I'm a Grown-Up Trapped in the Body of a Fifth Grader*. Instead Flora just said, "It's not so bad."

Zaidee had this fancy-looking salad in a white case with a glass top covering it.

"What is that?" Flora asked.

"Salade composeé," she said. Her French accent was perfect. It was so annoying how perfect Zaidee was. "It's a composed salad."

Now it was Flora's turn to act haughty. "I got that *salade* meant *salad*," Flora said.

Zaidee raised an eyebrow. One perfectly plucked eyebrow, like a whole two inches above her eyeball. What kid knows how to do that?

"Oh really?" she said. Then she rattled something off in a French that sounded extraordinarily snooty.

When Flora got home, she sent Clara an email:

Querida Clara,

There has been an invasion in our town of tall, perfect-looking robots. It's as if French-speaking department store mannequins have come to life and invaded the fifth grade. I have only met their leader, but she is terrifying, and the army of her type that is sure to follow may be the end of life in Westerly as we know it. My only happiness is that by moving, you have cleverly escaped her clutches. I do not know how many of us will survive.

Okay, that's an exaggeration. There's a new girl at school. She's a piece of work. Call me when you can.
Your forever friend,
Flora

CHAPTER 19

The Great Debate

The next morning when Flora woke up, there was an email from Clara. That was the one not terrible thing about the time difference between Westerly and San Francisco. If Flora emailed Clara at night, she could count on waking up to an email. It was like starting the day with a gift.

Hola and Holla!

I was horrified to hear that our town has been invaded by robots or one, too tall, too perfect, new girl at school bot. One question—any chance you can reprogram her? If we learned anything from Star Wars, it's that a sentient droid can come in mighty handy.

May the force be with you, Flora la Fresca.

Tu mejor amiga,

Clara

That morning, Flora got all dressed up in a white shirt, a gray bow tie that she borrowed from her dad, and a pleated skirt that she had not worn since her mother made her get all dressed up for their family's Día de los Reyes dinner. The skirt was itchier than she remembered, but she liked what she saw in the mirror. She was ready to take on Señorita Blazers.

Zaidee dressed as if every day was debate club. On this particular day, she was wearing a light blue shirt, a dark blue blazer, and off-white capri-length pants. Instead of her usual ballet slippers, she was wearing pumps with a little heel.

Geez Louise, Flora thought. *What kind of fifth grader wears heels?*

The school principal, Ms. Sargent, greeted the class, took a seat in the back of the room, and opened her notebook. Flora could feel herself sweating. The notebook was to decide points. The points would decide if she and her team won or lost. Flora wanted to win so bad that she felt a little woozy.

She had lost her best friend to California and a girl named Avery with whom she now ate all kinds of delicious food. Her parents thought her sister walked on water. In a year that had turned out to be terrible and horrible, Flora needed a win and she thought maybe, just maybe, this debate might be that win. She raised her hand and asked her teacher if she could go to the water fountain before they began. Mrs. Romano said it was okay. Then Zaidee raised her hand and said she wanted to go to the water fountain too. Geez Louise.

At the fountain, after they'd both taken more than a sip, Zaidee said, "Ugh, my throat is so dry. I guess I'm a little nervous."

It was a surprising statement because she didn't look nervous. At least Flora didn't think so.

"Why would you be jittery?" Flora asked. "You've done debate club before." Flora didn't say what she'd been thinking—that Zaidee was going to kick her rebuttal.

"Ever since we moved to the States, I've been self-conscious of my accent," Zaidee said.

This also sounded crazy. Everybody loved a French accent. At least that's what Flora thought. Zaidee continued, "In Europe, in Latin America, in Africa, there are lots of different kinds of accents. And since I always attended international schools, all the kids sounded different. Here, everyone sounds so much more alike. It's that American accent that you hear in all the TV shows and movies. You either have it or you don't. I definitely do not have it."

Mrs. Romano stuck her head out of the classroom. "Girls! We are waiting on you to begin."

As Flora walked back to the classroom, Zaidee's words spun around inside of her head. She never thought her American accent was anything special. At home, everybody had Panamanian accents, and she definitely didn't have that. She wondered if that wasn't just the way things were: You were always inside on some things and outside on others.

Flora began because the affirmative side always went first. She stood up and said, "Our team would like to begin by saying that the vending machines that are being addressed in this debate are mislabeled. Those machines offer caffeinated beverages, but they also sell energy drinks and sparkling water. I'd like to state that the salient matter is not one's opinions about a particular beverage, the issue on the table is freedom of choice and how the restriction of those freedoms goes against everything we are taught about living in a democracy."

Mrs. Romano nodded and then Zaidee stood up, reminding Flora how tall she was. Flora sighed. Her height somehow made everything she said sound more grown-up.

Zaidee argued that "Sodas are no better than cigarettes. Health is the matter at hand. Both drinking soda and smoking cigarettes share several startling outcomes: including weight gain, heart disease, and diabetes. The Centers for Disease Control reports in their most recent studies that over thirty-seven million people in the US have diabetes right now. That is almost one in ten of the population."

Zaidee was using statistics. Flora and her team hadn't researched the statistics. Flora felt very nervous.

Flora huddled her team and whispered to Niklas, "After you make your point, I'll ask her if she has the age statistics on diabetes. My guess is that it's for grown-ups, not for kids."

Daisy nodded approvingly. "Great idea, Flora."

Flora beamed. Even if they lost, she'd gotten props from the smartest girl in the school.

Niklas stood up and said, "Our team would like to point out that chocolate milk, which the school offers all students for free, has a lot of sugar. One cup of low-fat chocolate milk has twenty-five grams of sugar. A cup of soda has, on average, twenty-six grams of sugar. It's not important what you serve, it's important that we educate kids about how to make healthy choices. My mom's a nutritionist and she says there are very few bad foods, but there are lots of bad choices. I have soda only when I go to the movies. That's my choice. I drink chocolate milk once a week, also a choice. Vending machines don't reach into your wallet and take your money. Vending machines don't pour soda down your throat. They offer a choice."

Aditya stood up, cleared his throat, and said, "Ladies and gentlemen of the jury . . ."

A bunch of kids, including Flora, laughed. But Mrs. Romano said gently, "It's not a jury, Aditya."

Aditya smiled and said, "Of course not, it's a debate and let's get to it. Vending machines aren't just bad for your health. They highlight economic inequity between students. Some kids have lots of money to spend on vending machines. But some kids might want a soda, but they don't get an allowance, they don't have that kind of money. We'd like to argue that snacks brought from home not only tend to represent healthier choices, but they also make it more comfortable for kids who don't have the cash to spend on expensive vending machine snacks."

Flora thought he made a good point.

Flora looked at her watch and said, "I have ninety seconds left. I'd like to ask the opposing team a question."

Mrs. Romano looked down at the stopwatch on her desk. "That is correct. You have ninety seconds left. Go ahead."

Flora asked, "We'd like to ask the opposing team what the ages are of the people with diabetes they mentioned in their opening remarks."

Palmer was up next. She said, "Approximately two hundred thousand kids under the age of eighteen."

Daisy whistled. She was a really good whistler. "That's a lot."

Niklas was the last speaker on Flora's team. He fake dribbled his way to the front of the classroom and then pretended to hit a layup before beginning his remarks. Some of the kids clapped and cheered.

"The school vending machines provide an important income revenue for the Parent Teacher Association. The funds are used primarily to support after-school programs in sports and the arts. We believe that kids don't buy more soda because it's sold in schools. The kids who love soda will either bring it from home or buy it on the way to school. So why not allow students to support their school while they're drinking their beverage of choice?"

Then it was time for Palmer to get up and give the last remarks for the opposition. "Many of the kids in our school have ADHD, attention deficit hyperactivity disorder," she said. Then she looked around the classroom and said, "Some of you are mad hyper. You know who you are—"

Mrs. Romano interrupted her and said, "Palmer, don't."

Palmer looked pleased, as if Mrs. Romano had complimented her and not reeled her in. She said, "Soda is sugary and makes it hard for kids to concentrate and pay attention. We know it's bad for us. We should do better."

Flora didn't know how this debate was going to go. She didn't want to pretend that drinking soda was healthy. But she did think that it was about choice, income for the schools, and, she wasn't going to lie, she really, *really* wanted to win.

Her teacher stood up, "Flora, it's time for your closing statement."

Flora stood and gave her team a thumbs-up.

Flora's voice was shaking a little, but she took a deep breath and read her closing remarks: "In conclusion, we'd like to state that we believe the vending machines are more net positive than negative when it comes to the well-being of our students. We believe that ultimately, it's about choice. The good that is done by the income of the vending machines cannot be understated. Now when you fly a plane, there's a carbon emission tax that lets you lessen your footprint on the environment. We'd like to suggest that by helping to fund programs in the arts and sports, the machines lessen their negative imprint by contributing, in value, to our physical and emotional well-being."

Flora's hands were shaking by the end but Daisy started clapping when she put her index cards down and the other students quickly joined in.

Zaidee stood up and said, "We'd like to start by complimenting the affirming team on their persuasive argument. However, we think that there is no middle ground when it comes to our health and our future. Soda is harmful and addictive. It's best that the school does away with access to it on all fronts."

The Lucys began the applause for Zaidee. Flora and the rest of the students politely joined in.

"I couldn't have been happier with this first debate," Mrs. Romano said. "Both teams put forward considered, thought-provoking arguments. Let me confirm with Ms. Sargent about her take on which team made the stronger argument."

The two women stepped outside of the classroom for what seemed like an interminable period of time.

"I really don't want to lose," muttered Flora.

Niklas nodded. "Losing is the worst."

Daisy said, "I'm not worried, we got this."

The teacher and the principal returned to the room and Ms. Sargent addressed the class. "This was a tough one," she said. "I was tempted to declare this a tie because both teams really brought their A game to this debate."

Flora's heart sank. She hated when schools declared a bona fide contest a tie. As if kids weren't strong enough to take the bad news of losing.

But Ms. Sargent wasn't done. She said, "However . . . Mrs. Romano and I both believe that debate club is about making hard choices."

Great, Flora thought. *Now I get to lose fair and square.*

Ms. Sargent continued, "I should add . . . this debate does not decide the future of vending machines in our school. That's actually a matter for the school board, local government, and state officials. But the team that made the more compelling argument was the affirmative team: Flora, Daisy, and Niklas."

Flora and her team jumped to their feet and high-fived each other. Ms. Sargent handed them each a certificate and a bookstore gift card.

Flora couldn't believe it. Yes, her skirt was itching so bad that she felt like she was sitting in the sand in a bed of red ants. But unexpectedly, this had turned into a pretty good, not terribly awful day.

CHAPTER 20

Peanuts

The next day, Zaidee waited after class for Flora so that they could walk to lunch together.

Flora said, "Hey, what's up, Zaidee?"

Zaidee said, "I just wanted to say congrats again on the debate. You totally deserved to win. Can we eat lunch together?"

The Lucys, who were congregating in the hallway and applying lip gloss in Palmer's locker mirror, eyed this development with suspicion.

Palmer, who was generally considered the head Lucy, said, "Zaidee, you're more than welcome to join us for lunch. I'm sure Flo won't mind."

Flora glared at her, "Nobody calls me Flo."

Palmer ignored her. "Totally your call, Zaidee."

Zaidee smiled and said, "Thanks Palmer, I'm having

lunch with Flora today. And by the way, I'm new around here, but I hear that she hates to be called Flo."

As they walked away, Flora had to fight the impulse to give Zaidee a high five the way she would've if Clara had stood up for her that way. "Why'd you do that?" Flora asked. "No one ever says no to the Lucys."

Zaidee looked confused. "Why do you call them that?"

Flora said, "Because they're like the girl in Charlie Brown."

"Charlie Brown?" Zaidee asked, still confused.

Flora took out her phone and pulled up a GIF of Lucy pulling the ball away just as Charlie is about to kick it. Charlie went horizontal, then up in the air before landing flat on his back.

Zaidee laughed. "I know this cartoon! So you think those girls are like that, huh? You are probably not wrong."

They sat down at the table with Aidan and Aditya. They were talking about the Japanese competitive eater who had eaten ten Twinkies in sixty seconds, a new world record.

"It's impossible," Aidan said. "You can't even take the wrappers off of ten Twinkies in sixty seconds."

Aditya gave his brother an incredulous look. "Dude, they take the wrappers off for you before the contest even begins."

Flora took in Zaidee's outfit, a pair of skinny jeans, a pink button-down shirt, and a black blazer, along with a black pair of ballet slipper shoes.

It was more than a little unexpected, that a girl like Zaidee who dressed so froufrou and acted so prim and proper would so clearly want to hang out with Flora, who was none of those things. In fact, at that very moment, Flora was wearing her favorite sweatshirt that featured a girl with her hair in a bun and it said: *Messy Hair, Don't Care.* Then as if to prove the point, Flora's bun was especially messy, don't care-y.

They unwrapped their lunches. Zaidee had a ham and cheese on baguette, from the local French bakery, Choc-o-Pain. Flora recognized the wrapper. Flora had a beef empanada and a green salad with a strawberry vinaigrette. The salad was unnecessary, but her father, who made her lunches, sometimes felt better about life when there was something green on the plate.

Flora asked Zaidee, "Can I ask you a question?"

Zaidee said, "Sure."

Flora asked, "What's up with the blazers?" Her mother always said she had a tendency to be blunt.

Zaidee didn't seem fazed by the question. She explained that at her old school, they wore uniforms. "I loved it because I hate shopping, and with a uniform, you just wear the same thing every day. When I found out that this school had no uniform, my mom said, 'We'll just make our own.' So we went to the store and we bought five pairs of jeans, five blazers, and seven button-down shirts."

Then she grinned. "It takes me five minutes to get dressed in the morning."

Flora was impressed. She too hated shopping. But it did not take her five minutes to get dressed in the morning. Because she hated shopping and she never took her mother's offer to clean out her closet, it was a jumbled mess of clothing from the third to the fifth grade.

"Two follow-up questions," Flora said. "One, do you mind if I copy your uniform idea?"

Zaidee said, "Not at all."

Flora said, "Second question, do you mind if I call you Blazers? You know, as a nickname."

Zaidee looked down at herself and said, "I guess. I mean, there have been worse nicknames."

For the first time since Clara moved away, Flora was legit sad when the lunch bell rang. She wasn't sure where Zaidee fell on the BFF-ometer. But she was easy to talk to and far from boring.

Flora said, "Hey, do you want to meet after school and get some boba tea?"

Zaidee said, "I don't know what boba is. But I do like tea. I'll ask my mother if it's okay."

Flora smiled and said, "Cool, cool. But be warned, if you don't like boba, I will be judging you. Boba is life."

Zaidee smiled back. "Message received. Boba is life."

CHAPTER 21

Why Shopping with Big Sisters No Es Bueno

The following weekend, it was an unseasonably warm Westerly day. It was the last weekend in April, but it was in the high sixties and the sun beamed brightly.

"Look," Flora's mother said as she prepared breakfast. "Clarita has sent us some of the California sunshine."

Flora scowled. "More like your generation ruined the planet. The sunshine is evidence of uneven climate change and we are all doomed."

Her mother gave her shoulder a squeeze. "Ay, Flora, no seas tan negativa."

"How am I supposed to be positive when we barely have an ozone layer?" Flora grumbled. *And how am I supposed to be positive about my best friend being gone?*

Despite the fact that Flora was not in the mood for socializing, her family decided to have a barbecue. That Saturday morning, they prepped. Her mother made potato salad and seasoned the steaks. Her father was on the back porch, stirring sangria. Her tíos, Rogelio and Luca, were playing dominoes with some of the Panamanian cousins who had stopped by. Her abuela and Mr. Carter were inside, keeping an eye on her baby cousin, Fina, who was taking a nap.

Her tío Rogelio was wearing a baby-blue polo shirt and linen pants. Her tío Luca was wearing a knit sweater and knee-length linen shorts.

Rogelio said, "Flora, I'll give you five dollars if you can tell me what country dominoes are originally from."

Flora LOVED her uncle's quizzes and also that he always gave her cash even if she got the answer wrong. "Panama!" she said right away—the way Panamanians loved dominoes, it had to be from their homeland.

Her uncle smiled and shook his head. "Guess again."

She thought for a second. "Puerto Rico?"

"It doesn't begin with a P," he said.

Flora sighed. There were a lot of countries and she didn't know what to guess next. "Okay, I give up."

"China," her uncle said.

"Stop with the history and focus on the game," Tío Luca urged, playfully hitting Rogelio on the arm.

"Flora, querida, when you fall in love, make sure you find yourself a person who knows how to play dominoes. I've been teaching your tío for years, but . . ."

Tío Luca scowled. "Flora, my love, when you find your person, it would be good if they were a person who abided by one set of rules when it came to a game like dominoes."

All the men around the table laughed because it was true; Tío Rogelio had been known to bend the rules as they suited him.

"I don't cheat!" Rogelio said. "What do I do, Flora?"

Flora grinned. "My tío does not cheat. He engages in an expansive and evolving conversation about what the rules could be."

"Just like I taught you," Rogelio said, slipping her a five-dollar bill.

"Since this game is over," Tío Luca said, "why don't you show me what you've been learning in dance class."

Flora and Luca walked to the side of the house and Flora showed him what she'd learned in class with Maylin. She was in such a zone doing the slides and body rolls, Flora was almost surprised when Tío Luca clapped and said, "Girl, you are on fire. You look amazing."

Flora took a sip from her water bottle and said, "Thank you!"

Maylin came over and said, "You missed like five steps, Flora. It's a good thing that you're not actually one of my damas, because—"

Flora didn't think, it just happened. She threw a tiny bit of water, all that was left in her water cup, in Maylin's face.

She knew it was bad.

But here's the thing: In the moment, it didn't feel bad at all. It felt *stupendous*.

The minute Flora did it, she instantly felt better. She had recently seen the musical *Hamilton* with her class.

It had bothered her so much—that terrible duel scene with Alexander Hamilton and Aaron Burr. If only Burr had thrown fizzy water in Hamilton's face, he would have felt the sweet satisfaction of punishing his foe without murdering anyone at all.

She was so deep in the reverie of how she, Flora la Fresca, could fix history that she hadn't noticed that even though there had been only the teeniest amount of water in the cup, Maylin had started screaming and. Would. Not. Stop.

"Come on Mayley Monster, *cálmate*," Flora said. She called Maylin that sometimes when her parents were out of earshot, as they had expressly asked her not to refer to her sister in such a derogatory manner.

Flora's mother came running from the screened-in porch. "Ay, niña," she said, gathering Maylin in her arms. "¿Qué pasó?"

Maylin cried and sputtered as if Flora had slugged her. And the way her sister was hamming it up, as if she were in bona fide pain, like a telenovela actress in the face of relentless tragedy, made Flora want to kick her in the shin, hard.

"She threw a cup of water. Right. In. My. Face," Maylin said.

"Flora, no," her mother said, her face a mixture of shock and horror.

"It was nothing, like *three* drops of water," Flora said.

"Unacceptable," her mother said. "Go to your room until your father and I figure out your punishment."

An hour later Flora's father knocked on the door. "Flora la Fresca," he said. "Why do you keep getting yourself into these kinds of pickles?"

It was a funny expression. Get yourself in a pickle. Flora had to resist the urge to laugh.

Her father sighed. "You shouldn't have thrown water in your sister's face. That was more than fresca. That was mean."

Flora wanted to explain that the cup was almost empty. There couldn't have been more than *five* drops of fizzy water in there. Twenty drops *tops*. She wanted to explain the moment of pure peace she had felt the minute she'd thrown the water. She wanted her dad to know how a little water in the face as a method of revenge might have saved Alexander Hamilton's life because nobody cared. Nobody understood.

It was one thing that Maylin's every waking hour was consumed with planning her quince, which was still two months away. It was quite another that Flora was roped into this web of crystallized rock candy lollipops, diamante headbands, and satin pouch party favors.

The next morning after breakfast, Flora's father, who was nobody's fool, announced that he needed to go into the shop to work on a custom order. "Sorry to leave you ladies," he said, winking at Flora.

"No hay problema," Flora's mother said, absentmindedly scrolling through a long list of to-dos on her phone.

"Oh! I want to go to the office with Papá," Flora said.

Flora's father gave her a look that said he was well aware that she was trying to glom on to his perfectly crafted escape.

"I could sharpen pencils!" she offered.

Her father said, "All of our pencils are in tip-top shape."

"I could scan plans for filing." Flora had just learned how to use the flatbed scanner and she was convinced that surely that was a useful, helpful skill.

"*Hija*," her mother said. "We could really use your help."

Flora wasn't against being helpful. "Just please tell me we're not going dress shopping."

Maylin, who had not looked up from her phone during the whole meal, said, "Of course we're going dress shopping. We are T minus eight weeks out from my quince and I don't even have my dress. It may need altering. The one I pick may be back ordered. Who knows what the deal will be?"

"But why do you need me?"

Flora's mother said, "Because Maylin is your sister and sisters look out for each other."

Flora had to fight the urge to laugh in her mother's house. When did Maylin ever look out for her?

Maylin was more honest. "Look here, flaca. It's my

quince and I need you to be there in case you might be helpful. Punto. That's the end of it."

Flora stepped out of the room and silent-screamed like Simba in *The Lion King*. Misery. Pure misery.

It wasn't that Flora didn't like going to the mall. What she disliked was shopping. It was totally cool to run into the mall and pick up free samples at the fancy food shop. She liked the movie theater at the mall. You could reserve seats and they would bring the food right to you, like you were in a restaurant, except you were at the movies. Flora thought that was pretty wonderful. There was a sporting goods shop at the mall and a discount store that sold everything from groceries to very affordable clothes. Flora's mother bought all her clothes for summer camp at the discount store because as she put it, "Flora was growing like a weed."

But Flora had managed to avoid the mall since Clara had moved. The whole place felt like a big old piggy bank of Clara memories.

Add to that, Flora knew as well as she knew her own name that shopping with Maylin was a unique form of torture. Most people, it seemed to Flora, shop with the express purpose of purchasing an item and leaving. Maylin shopped in another way entirely. She rarely bought anything, but shopping with her could still take hours.

It's important to know that while some kids exaggerate about time, Flora was not one of those kids. She loved adventure and spontaneity, but she also valued punctuality. She had gotten her first watch in second grade. In third grade, she got an alarm clock in the shape of a princess movie she once loved but would come to loathe. But ever since she received that alarm clock, she woke herself up in the morning and she never hit snooze. She prided herself on being on time for things, and when her mother gave her the tiniest bit of freedom, like letting her walk to the boba store by herself as long as she was back in thirty minutes, Flora made sure she was back in twenty-five.

So when she said that Maylin had the capacity to arrive at the mall and leave hours later without purchasing a single thing, she meant it. This meant that Maylin's shopping was now *everybody's* problem.

If Flora were her mother, she would have made Maylin pick a dress or she would have picked it out herself. But her mother kept saying that "it's your sister's special day, ten paciencia."

Somehow, Maylin had gotten it into her head that the mere fact that she was getting a year older meant that she was now more important than ever, like a movie star or something. She swooped into the fanciest store in the mall and immediately began tearing through the racks as if she were looking for something to wear to the Oscars. She held dresses up to herself in the mirror. She texted photos of the dresses to her friends, then sat on the fancy chaise longue in the dressing area, waiting for her friends to text back. She held up dresses to her mother, asking her opinion. Then she declared that "nobody understands me" when her mother favored a dress she didn't like.

After forty-five of the longest minutes in Flora's life, Maylin stepped into the dressing room with three dresses that seemed identical, except in color.

Her sister's indecisiveness was making Flora loca. She said, "They all look alike. Pick one and let's go home."

"Are you kidding me?" Maylin said. "These dresses are nothing alike. This one has a cold shoulder sleeve, and I really need to show off my arms. Varsity volleyball has got me ripped. I've worked hard for these guns."

Maylin flexed her muscles and Flora pretended to vomit all over the dressing room floor. She was really good at making vomiting sounds, so much so that the two women waiting for a dressing room looked a little sick.

"Flora Violeta Yara Castillo LeFevre!" her mother said. "You stop that right now."

Flora grinned, proud of herself. Her mother only used her full name when she wanted to get her attention. It was meant to be a punishment, but Flora loved hearing all five of her names, called out in her mother's singsongy Panamanian accent. It made her feel like a legend, like the hero of a book or a movie.

Maylin emerged again from the dressing room and

did a little twirl. She admired herself in the mirror as if staring at the most beautiful painting in the world. *Who does that?* Flora thought. She knew that self-esteem was important, but Maylin looked like she wanted to kiss her own image in the mirror. So weird.

"What do you think, Mami?" Maylin asked.

Then before their mother could answer, Maylin said, "The jewel-beaded bodice is beautiful, but maybe it's a little OTT?"

Flora guffawed. *Everything* about Maylin was OTT, over the top.

A few minutes later, Maylin emerged from the dressing room in a pouffy yellow dress that made her look like Big Bird.

"This looked so pretty on the hanger, but now I'm not sure," Maylin said, looking uncharacteristically insecure.

Their mother said, "Try it with the crown. It could work. It's got a carnival vibe that reminds me of celebrations in Panama."

Maylin took the sparkly crown with yellow crystals

and feathers. "I respect our Indigenous heritage, but I don't know about the crystals and feathers."

"Wear the feathers!" Flora said, her smile widening.

"Um, okay," Maylin said, and put the crown on. "¿Qué piensas, Mami?"

The sight of Maylin swathed in electric-yellow taffeta and feathers was so funny, Flora all of a sudden was thrilled she hadn't opted out of the shopping trip. Her sister looked *ridiculous*. Moreover, she didn't seem to realize it. Which meant that there was a chance Maylin would buy this monstrosity of a dress and wear it to her quince. *That* meant the whole entire enterprise would be like a giant sketch comedy show. Oh, Flora thought, that would be fun. That would be *good*.

As Maylin and their mother appraised the Big Yellow Pouf as if it were a legitimate option, Flora started to giggle. Once she started, she couldn't stop. She slumped to the floor.

Maylin flushed and looked genuinely upset. "Are you laughing at me?"

"No, I'm laughing *with* you," Flora said, laughing

harder. "We can all agree that dress is giving you serious *Sesame Street* vibes."

Flora's mother said, "This is Maylin's choice. Whatever she chooses, she has our full support."

It was all the affirmation Maylin needed. She took a deep breath, adjusted her feathered crown, and said, "The thing is, yellow is my power color. The astrologer who did my chart last week at the mall said so."

Flora's mother said, "Maybe we can look at a softer yellow, more of a butter yellow."

Maylin took the dress off and handed it to Flora. "See if they have this in butter yellow."

Flora took the dress and pretended to curtsy. "Yes, m'lady. And the crown?"

Maylin said, "I'm keeping this. I kind of like it. Now scoot."

"Is *please* even part of your vocabulary?" Flora asked.

Maylin ignored her.

Flora turned to her mother. "Doesn't she have to say please?"

Her mother, however, had not been paying attention. "I'm sure she said it," she said, staring at her phone. "Your sister has impeccable manners. Darn it. This text is from the caterers. Let me step out and call them."

Flora nodded. Deep down inside, she knew her mother was kind of amazing. But she and Maylin were so alike that sometimes it didn't feel like Flora fit in with them.

When she got home, she sent Clara a text.

Buenos fiascos, Clara.

A few minutes later, she got a response.

Buenos fiascos, Flora. What's the latest?

Flora smiled. "Buenos fiascos" was one of those funny things that only Clara would ever say. Clara used to say, "Come on Flora, you got to admit. Fiascos are so much more buenos than días."

Flora wanted to type *I miss you. I'm lonely. Everything is worse since you moved away.* But she didn't want to seem like a drag. She wanted Clara to remember her as a fun friend, not a sad one.

Why did the skateboarder go to a movie? Flora texted.

After a few seconds Clara typed, *I dunno. Tell me, Fresca.*

Because he was wheely board.

Flora smiled to herself, knowing that Clara would appreciate the joke.

A few seconds later, she got three laugh-cry emojis. Success, she thought. Sometimes just telling a joke that makes your best friend laugh is the best you can hope for.

CHAPTER 23

The Problem With Treating Teenagers Like Royalty

The next day, after school, Flora and Zaidee met up at the front gate. Zaidee was wearing a green blazer. Flora said, "Nice blazer, Blazers."

As they walked down Bay Street, Zaidee said, "I'm glad you're here to show me around. It's hard being new."

Flora said, "There's not much to show. This is a teeny-tiny town. Everything is on this one street."

Flora had learned that although Zaidee had most recently lived in Paris, she had been born in Lebanon and lived there until the second grade.

"What is Lebanon like?" Flora asked.

"Beirut is a magical place," Zaidee said. "It's full of contrasts. Everything is old, some of the villas are hundreds of years old. There are so many different flowers and you can turn one way and find yourself walking down a cobblestone street with little shops and restaurants and turquoise-blue shutters that mirror the color of the beaches. But then another street, there might be a door full of bullet holes and you are reminded, in an instant, of how many wars have been fought on these streets."

Flora was having a hard time picturing it. "You'll have to show me pictures. I'd like to see."

Zaidee asked, "What is Panama like?"

Flora was embarrassed to say that she had never been. Most of her extended family now lived in Rhode Island. "There's no one left to visit," her mother had once said. "So there's not as much reason to go."

Flora told Zaidee, "I'd like to see the places where my mom grew up and where my parents met. I'll go someday . . . Sometimes I feel like our house is like a little embassy. When you step in the door, it's like we're in a little corner of Panama. Especially on Sunday nights when we have a big family dinner, the food is Panamanian, the accents are Panamanian, the music and the smells are all Panama. At least, some version of it that my parents carry with them."

Zaidee smiled and said, "It's like that for us too. There's a Middle Eastern spice called za'atar; there are different blends but they all have a mixture of thyme, salt, sumac, and sesame seeds. Whenever we have friends or family come visit, they always bring us a jar from wherever they are coming from—Jordan, Beirut, or Palestine. It always smells to me like sunshine and the Mediterranean and family picnics by the sea. That's one of the things I like about Westerly. It smells like the sea."

Flora smiled. Loving the smell of the sea was definitely worth a point on the BFF-ometer, and so was knowing about cool, fancy spices.

Flora stopped in front of a storefront that had a big mural of Bruce Lee, the martial arts legend, striking a karate pose. "We're here," she said. "Welcome to Bruce Lee Boba."

"I've heard of boba, but I've never tried it," Zaidee said, peering into the shop.

They stood outside, looking at the menu. Flora

explained that boba tea was like a Taiwanese milk-shake. She showed Zaidee the list with all the flavors: green tea, mango, strawberry, passion fruit, grape-fruit.

Zaidee looked dubious. "What's in the little black balls?"

Flora said, "They are *delicious*. They are made of tapi-oca."

Zaidee said, "What's tapioca?"

Flora said, "It's like a pudding."

Zaidee looked like she didn't even want to try it. "Are they squishy?"

Flora beamed. "So squishy!"

Zaidee grimaced. "I hate squishy things."

Flora said, "Who doesn't like squishy things? What kind of monster are you?"

Even though Flora had called her a monster, Zaidee laughed. "What else can I have here at Bruce Lee Boba?"

Flora looked around. "There's Ramune." She pointed to the mini fridge with bottles of all different colors. "It's a kind of soda."

Zaidee said, "I'll try that."

After a few more minutes of deliberation, Flora settled on a passionfruit boba and Zaidee chose the Blue Hawaii Ramune.

Ramune was a Japanese soda with a marble at the neck of the bottle. "You press the marble into the bottle," Flora said. "Then you chug, chug, chug."

Zaidee followed the instructions and took a sip. "I think I may have to disagree with you. Ramune is life. Can I keep the marble at the end? It's so pretty."

Flora shook her head and said, "Nope."

Zaidee didn't understand. "Why?"

Flora explained, "I once saw a video of a dad trying to take the marble out of a Ramune bottle. Dude used a mini chainsaw. There were shards of glass everywhere. So not worth it."

Zaidee agreed, "Totally not worth it."

Flora said, "So tell me more about where you're from."

Zaidee said, "We've moved a lot. Lebanon, it's a funny place. We've been at war, on and off, for hundreds of years. So we are—as my parents like to put it—nomadic. When things are good, we go home. When they are bad, my parents find another job and we move."

Flora said, "That sounds exciting. I've only ever lived in this boring little town."

"It is and it isn't exciting," Zaidee explained. "So far we've lived in France, Senegal, and Mexico City, CDMX. All beautiful places, but every time I start to feel settled, we move again."

Flora said, "Mexico City, so you speak Spanish."

"Not really," Zaidee said. "I went to a French school, the Lycée Franco-Mexicain in CDMX, but I picked up a little. Pero like . . . poquito, poquito."

Flora couldn't wait to tell Clara. She'd finally met a friend who spoke two additional languages, French *and* Arabic.

"So, tell me about Paris," Flora asked.

"We actually lived outside the city in a town called Versailles."

Flora had never heard of it.

Zaidee's eyes widened. "Really? It's famous because it has this sick palace there. The Palais de Versailles."

Flora was intrigued. "I think we need some macarons to go with this conversation."

Zaidee said, "They sell macarons here? What an intriguing place. Taiwanese milkshakes, Japanese sodas, French pastries."

Flora said, "Intriguing is how I roll. And you've got to teach me how to pronounce macarons the way you do. Your French accent is off the hook."

She went up to the counter and returned with a plate of macarons, the figure of Bruce Lee emblazoned on the plate.

"What does Bruce Lee have to do with boba?" Zaidee asked.

"Absolutely nothing," Flora said. "But he's sure fun to watch." Besides providing the main motif for the illustrations that were emblazoned across the plates, cups, and napkins, there were two TV screens that showed a nonstop series of Hong Kong action movies.

Flora pointed down to the plate. "We've got green tea, Nutella, Earl Grey, coconut, chocolate, and these blue ones."

Zaidee took a blue macaron and said, "Do you know

they call the blue ones Marie Antoinette macarons?"

Flora did not.

"Well, Marie Antoinette was a diva of the highest order," Zaidee explained. "She became the future queen of France when she was just fifteen years old."

Flora said, "My sister, Maylin, is about to be fifteen, and she thinks she's the queen of Westerly."

Zaidee said, "Still, it must be nice to have a big sister. Being an only means I spend *way* too much time with my parents."

Flora said, "Just the opposite. She makes my life a misery. But enough about her. Tell me about the fifteen-year-old princess."

"Well, she became queen of France when she was nineteen," Zaidee continued. "And by all accounts, she was a spoiled brat. Most of France was really poor, but she spent obscene amounts of money on over-the-top ball gowns and jewelry. She had a posse of obnoxious girlfriends who were like her ladies-in-waiting. They just lived to dress up and indulge themselves."

"Wow," Flora said. "She's just like my sister."

Flora knew her sister was the worst. She hadn't known that Maylin had such a stunning historical precedent. "Okay," Flora said. "New code name for my she-beast sister: MA, short for Marie Antoinette."

Zaidee said, "You love giving people nicknames. But what about you? Do you have one?"

Flora said, "My friend Clara used to call me Flora la Fresca."

Zaidee said, "Because you drink Fresca?"

"No, because I like to make my own rules and sometimes grown-ups think I'm a little bit rude."

"A little bit rude is okay, don't you think?" Zaidee said. "Especially if you're a girl, it's important not to be a doormat. Sometimes if you're nice, people stomp all over you. My mother always says 'Don't mistake kindness for weakness' when people try to push her around. "

"Oooh, I like it," Flora said, slurping the bubbles at the bottom of her bubble tea.

Zaidee made a face. "I can hear how squishy those things are."

Flora didn't want to be rude. She stopped sucking up boba bubbles with her straw. "I can finish it at home—if you want."

"That's nice of you to stop your slurping, just because

of me," Zaidee said, sincerely. "But you should finish it. I'm just happy you pointed me in the Ramune direction. I think boba is not for me."

"Fair enough," Flora said. "So you ever see Marie Antoinette prancing around your town in France?"

"Of course not. She lived *hundreds* of years ago. Do you want to know how she died?" Zaidee whispered.

Flora's eyes glittered. She absolutely *did* want to know how the spoiled teenage queen perished.

"How'd she die?" Flora asked, whispering back.

Zaidee leaned in and said, "She died on the *guillotine*."

Flora did not know what that was, but everything Zaidee said in French sounded so nice.

Zaidee sensed immediately that Flora had not grasped the full implication of Marie Antoinette's tragic end.

"Flora," she asked, "do you know what a guillotine is?"

Flora admitted that she did not.

"It's a machine that cuts off your head." Zaidee mimicked lying down on the table, then looked up. "You lie down like this," she continued. "Then a giant blade comes crashing down and *voilà*, your head is severed from your body; you are super-duper dead."

This Flora liked a lot.

"It's where the expression 'Heads will roll' comes from," Zaidee explained. "Because in the old days if you got in trouble, out came the guillotine, and your head would roll away from your body."

"Wow," Flora said. "That is awful. And awesome. And gruesome. Awesomely gruesome."

Zaidee smiled. "Do you know what else I learned in Versailles?"

Flora could not wait to hear.

"It was rumored that the ghost of Marie Antoinette remained a shopaholic, even after her death."

"No!"

"Oui, oui. It is said that in the fanciest boutiques in Paris, there have been glimpses of Marie Antoinette, walking around headless in a bloody ball gown, holding a head that is still perfectly made up with red lips and flawlessly curled ringlets."

Flora could picture the bratty, teenage headless queen and it frightened her, just a little bit. "That's horrifying," she said.

"But there's more," Zaidee said conspiratorially.

Flora nodded excitedly.

"It is said that sometimes when you are in the dressing room of a shop, all by yourself, you would suddenly feel a cold chill on your neck. Then you'd hear a raspy, ghostly voice say, 'Pretty dress, dear. You should absolutely buy that one.'"

Flora squealed. Mrs. Oh, who owned the boba shop, walked over and said kindly, "Keep it down, girls."

"And *that* is why I hate shopping," Zaidee said, beaming.

"I am done! I am so done!" Flora said. "That is the best ghost story I have ever heard."

It felt good to laugh so hard. Flora had to admit that Zaidee was becoming a real friend—it was nice to have someone to sit with at lunch and hang out with after school.

Flora hadn't thought it was possible, after Clara had moved away. But it was what Mrs. Romano always said: Life likes to be surprising.

CHAPTER 23

Zaidee's House

The next week, Zaidee invited Flora to do homework at her house after school. Flora knew that this meant their friendship was going to a new level. It was one thing to have lunch at school or even to go out for boba. But hanging out at each other's houses was a precursor to sleepovers. Flora felt both guilty and curious. Did this mean she was over missing Clara? Is this how Clara and Avery's friendship had begun?

Zaidee's house was beautiful, like something out of a magazine. It had a flat roof and giant windows on every side. Zaidee said the style was called "mid-century modern." The backyard of her house sloped down to a river, and there was a huge tire swing and a greenhouse that had a dining table and lots of plants. "Sometimes," Zaidee explained, "my parents have fancy dinners in that greenhouse. But mostly I do my homework out there and make up plays about Venus flytraps that mutate and take over the world.

"Do you want to see it?" Zaidee asked.

Flora nodded.

"Follow me."

The greenhouse consisted of two parts. One was a traditional greenhouse with rows of beautiful plants and flowers.

In the second room, there was a dining table and living room. Flora thought it seemed like a real life magic treehouse, the way the glass-domed ceiling cast rays of sunlight and shadows of the trees above onto the gray slate floor.

"Oh my gosh, it's so warm and cozy in here," Flora said, flopping onto an oversized armchair covered in a botanical pattern.

Zaidee threw her bookbag on the floor and sat on the couch opposite Flora. "It's so good, right?" she said. "My baba says that what's good for the plants is good for us."

At that moment, her father came into the room and said, "Are you quoting me, Zaidee?"

He put his hand on his chest and said, "Ahlan, Zaidee. Marhaba, you must be Zaidee's new friend, Flora."

Flora blushed, both surprised and happy that Zaidee had actually told her father about her.

"Nice to meet you . . ."

Flora didn't know what to call him.

He smiled at her, with eyes that were large and deeply sunk in. His face had a hint of sadness to it, but the moment he smiled, his eyes danced. "You can call me Professor Khal."

"You will stay for tea, Flora?" he asked.

"I will," she said, trying not to be gobsmacked by the grown-up fanciness of it all.

A few minutes later, Professor Khal returned with a pot and delicate china cups covered in a pattern of painted leaves and ferns.

"Cinnamon rose tea," he explained as he poured the girls each a cup. "And baklava."

Zaidee beamed. "My mother makes these herself. My favorite is the orange-scented ones."

Flora took a bite of the pastry that Zaidee handed her. It was different from anything she had ever tasted before. And for a moment, she felt like she was betraying Clara. She wasn't in her father's shop, texting her best friend. She was having tea and sweets in a fancy greenhouse.

"Call me if you need more tea," Professor Khal said. "I'll be working in the other room."

He left and Flora said, "Your dad is nice. And this greenhouse is insanely beautiful."

Zaidee sighed. "It's a beautiful house and this is a very nice town, but it isn't home. We go home to

Lebanon for a month or two every year, but we never stay. Baba says we must follow the work. But what that means is we are always living someplace where people don't look or sound like me."

"All of my mother's family is here in the States, so we never go back to Panama," Flora explained. "My

sister is always lording it over me that she lived there before I was born and that's why her Spanish accent is so flawless. I'd love to go back for a month, see what it's like. My mother and father act like it's the perfect place."

Zaidee shrugged. "That's just what immigrant parents do. They have to make the past seem more perfect than it is. That's how they survive the hard work of making a life in a new country."

"Tell me more about Beirut. I'm going to be perfectly honest and tell you I'd never even heard of the city until you told me about it."

Zaidee smiled. "It's a little like New York, a little like Paris, and really like nowhere else in the world. There's a hum to the city; you feel it the moment you land, and it stays with you until you leave. My mother says that because people know how hard life can get, they are obsessed with joy. From the moment we arrive to the moment we leave, friends and family throw parties for us, just because. There's always delicious food, and dancing, and I get to stay up way later than I do in any other place."

Flora was a little jealous. Her bedtime, eight p.m. for a fifth grader, seemed exceptionally ridiculous to her.

"That sounds like the opposite of this place," she said. "Living in a small town can be so aburrido. Boring with a capital B."

Zaidee laid her long, tall-like-a-grown-up legs out on the couch. "I dunno," she said. "Boring can be comforting. My parents like it here. My father says it reminds him of a snow globe his father once brought him from London, of a village on the sea where none of the buildings were taller than the lowest star in the night sky."

"That's beautiful, Z," Flora said.

"Beirut is very different, but like Westerly, it's on the sea. My mother says the Atlantic isn't like the Mediterranean, but when she walks on the beach and closes her eyes, even on a cold day—"

"It smells like home," Flora said, smiling.

"Yeah," Zaidee said, eyeing her new friend with interest. "How'd you know?"

"My uncle Rogelio says the same thing. Even though

Westerly is nothing, I mean nada, not even an iota, like Panama, my uncle said that because there was plenty of work, and the sea is right here, he knew this could be a good home for our family."

CHAPTER 24

Ghostbusters

Every weekend, Flora's family had movie night. They took turns choosing a movie and everyone had to watch—no moaning, no complaining, and, "This is important," as her mother put it: no devices.

That Saturday, Flora's dad had chosen the original *Ghostbusters*, which had been one of his favorite movies when he was growing up.

A few months before, their mother had chosen the all-female *Ghostbusters*, which they all had found very funny. So much so that Flora had added "paranormal research" to the list of things she wanted to do when she grew up.

As her father hit play on the movie, Flora noticed that Maylin was staring at her phone as if it were welded to her hand. She stared at it as if she were a big-time banker and was making *millions* like the stockbroker in that movie her father loved but said the girls were too young to watch.

Flora's dad reached out to touch her phone and said, "Caramba niña, feel your phone—it's burning up because you never put it down."

Her mother added, "The health implications of that can't be good."

Maylin said, "Why do I have to put my phone down when Flora is on her iPad?"

Flora hated it when Maylin tried to drag her into her sphere of drama. Flora didn't use her tablet to text her friends or scroll through gossipy celebrity sites. She used her iPad to draw. Watching movies and drawing went perfectly together like peanut butter and pancakes, which, incidentally, was Flora's favorite breakfast food.

She could tell her parents were going to side with the Maylin Monster. They exchanged glances as if by telepathically looking at each other, they could land on the right decision.

"As much as I hate it . . ." Flora's mother began.

"A device is a device," her father said.

"So put the tablet away," her mother continued.

Maylin smiled and Flora thought, fine. Flora-2, Maylin-1.

Flora had found the original *Ghostbusters* to be less funny and more like a documentary about how bad special effects used to be when her parents were young. But for some reason, Maylin found the old-school special effects to be super scary.

"Oh my god, make it stop!" she said, freaking out when the cards in the library card catalog started flying all over the place.

Flora thought the slime and the big showdown with the gargoyles and the red-eyed ghosts on the roofs was hilarious.

But Maylin jumped up and said, "I have to go to the bathroom."

Flora heard her lock the powder room door and she proceeded not to come out for another twenty minutes, which feels like forever when you're watching a movie.

Flora suspected Maylin was in the bathroom texting,

which was, in Flora's opinion, not just gross but rude.

Maylin did not get in trouble because Maylin hardly ever got in trouble, for anything. But when the movie was done, Maylin all-too-casually asked, "Hey Flora, do you want to have a sleepover in my room?"

And at that moment, Flora knew her big sister had been legit scared.

Flora said yes because she hardly ever got to see the inside of Maylin's room, which was like a picture from a catalog with framed artwork and a fancy dressing table with a mirror that lit up that Maylin called a vanity.

When they changed into their pajamas, and Flora was settled into the trundle bed that Maylin used for sleepovers, Flora said, "Let's play two truths and a lie."

Maylin made a face and said, "Ugh, let's not."

Then she rolled over and within minutes, Maylin was snoring. Flora's sister was snoring so loudly that Flora was sure she wasn't faking it. So Flora rolled over and went to sleep too.

✳ ✳ ✳

The next morning, when Flora woke up, Maylin came in, fresh from the shower. She wore a short terry cloth robe and her hair was wet.

"Okay, get out," Maylin said.

"But why?" Flora asked, holding on to the smallest shred of hope that she and Maylin might actually have a sisterly moment.

"Because I'm going to blow-dry my hair," Maylin said.

"Why can't I sit here?"

"Because I need my privacy," Maylin snarled. "Vete."

"I thought maybe we could do something today," Flora said. "Like go to a movie?"

Maylin looked offended. Like she hadn't been totally spooked at the movie the night before.

"I have to go shopping for my quince dress," she said. "And when I want to go to a movie, I'll go with my actual friends."

Flora wanted to say something. Something fresco that would be a clever comeback. But she couldn't think. She rushed out of Maylin's room before her sister could see the tears that Flora could feel were coming.

When she got to her room, she picked up her phone

to text Clara and couldn't believe her eyes. There was a photo of Clara and Avery holding up her map, the one she had made by hand as a gift for Clara. They were standing at the entrance to the Golden Gate Bridge, the one she'd spent so much time researching and had drawn, she thought, to perfection.

She went down to the kitchen, where her father was making coffee.

"Look at this!" she said, her face a mess of tears.

"Oh Flora," her father said, pulling her in for a hug. "Is that the map you made for Clara?"

Flora nodded. "Now she's visiting all of those places with her new awful friend. The girl doesn't even rank on the BFF-ometer."

"I guess that's what they call a bridge too far," her father said.

"What?" Flora asked.

"Just making a silly joke," he murmured. "I'm sure she sent the picture because she wanted you to know how much she loved your gift. Not because she was trying to hurt your feelings."

"But she did. She did hurt my feelings."

Her father hugged her tighter and even though she knew she wasn't alone, she had never felt more like Flora la Sola.

CHAPTER 25

A Well-Deserved Haunting

Flora had thought her life was looking up. She was loving her dance classes so much that her tíos had promised to take her into New York to see a performance by Alvin Ailey if her final report card had all B's or higher, which was going to be easy peasy lemon squeezy. Zaidee was no Clara, but at least she was a friend.

But the whole thing where she was being recruited to be her sister's servant was getting ridiculous.

Her mother had insisted that Flora go with them to the mall. "The quince is less than a month away," she said. "We need all the help we can get. Las hermanas se cuidan unas a otras."

While their mother took a call from the hospital, Flora and Maylin went back to the dressing room with an armful of dresses the sales assistant had put aside for her.

"I need you to be a good little assistant," Maylin said, handing Flora her purse and water bottle as she entered the dressing room.

Flora put them both on the floor next to the chair.

"Flora, ¿estás loca?" Maylin screeched so loudly that several of the people turned around to look. "Don't put my purse on the floor. You know that's bad luck."

It was true. It was Panamanian superstition that if you put your bag on the floor, all your money would magically disappear. But Flora had forgotten.

Maylin stepped out of the dressing room in a horrible-looking burgundy satin dress.

"I like this one," she said, taking her phone out and taking a photo of herself in the dressing room mirror. "Let me text my girls and see what they think.

"Hand me my water," she said, not even looking at Flora.

"Can you say please?"

"Por favor, babosa," Maylin growled.

Babosa was not a nice word and Flora had the urge to

throw the water all over Maylin. It would be fitting considering her horrible-looking witchy dress.

Flora wasn't sure what made her look up. But when she did, she realized the walls of the dressing room did not go all the way up. For that matter, they did not go all the way down. The walls between the dressing rooms weren't really walls at all. They were partitions.

Interesting, she thought. *Very interesting.*

Then it occurred to her. What if she could convince Maylin that the dressing room was haunted? That would knock her off her quince princesa pedestal.

Flora remembered how scared Maylin had been when they watched *Ghostbusters*, plus the scary story Zaidee had told her about the young, fashion-crazed queen and her beheading. If she could conjure the ghost of Marie Antoinette, then maybe it would teach Maylin once and for all that Flora was her sister, not her servant.

It would have remained just a thought if the saleswoman, whose name tag read *Trish*, hadn't said, "We're getting a whole new line of dresses in this week. They're designed by the singer Rosalía. Only five stores on the East Coast are carrying them, and we are one of them. If you want, I can put a hold on all the dresses in your size."

Maylin's eyes widened. "That would be wonderful."

Then she turned to Flora and said, "We're done here. Hang up all of these dresses."

"OMG," Flora said. "Do you even know how to say please?"

Their mother turned to Trish and said, "We'll be back next Saturday."

Flora grinned. That gave her six whole days to make her move.

Clara would have been the perfect partner in crime for this prank. But Clara was in California and, last Flora had checked on Clara's Instagram, discovering the joy of Japanese tacos made with nori seaweed shells with her new friend Avery.

Flora needed an accomplice. But who? Blazers had turned out to be cooler than expected, but could she be counted on to follow Flora down the dastardly rabbit hole of Prankville?

Like her mother always said, "No pierdes nada en preguntar." And it was Blazers who had told her the cool story about the ghost of Marie Antoinette.

The next day, after school, Flora asked Zaidee if she could talk to her.

Sitting on the benches near the bus line, Flora explained that she wanted to pull a very innocent but fun prank on her sister.

"I'm in," Zaidee said enthusiastically.

After school, they walked together to Bruce Lee Boba. After they had both ordered, they settled into what had become their favorite table near the window.

Zaidee unrolled a piece of paper with little blue squares.

"Whoa," Flora said. "What in the name of blazers is that?"

"Blueprint paper," Zaidee explained. "My father took a garden architecture course and he had some left over. You talk and I'll sketch out the plan."

Zaidee took out a perfectly sharpened pencil and Flora talked the plan through.

"All the dressing rooms are in a row," Flora said, as Zaidee sketched. "But in between them, there's a gap at the top and the bottom."

"Like this?" Zaidee said, showing her the drawing.

"Exactly," Flora said. "I downloaded this app called Sound More Spooky. It records your voice and plays it back in a scary distorted way. You can use it to sound like a ghost or an ogre or a zombie."

Flora showed Zaidee the app and Zaidee said, "Oooh, I like this one."

She tapped an icon and then whispered, "You should be very afraid." And Flora had to admit, even though she was looking right at Zaidee, her voice sounded so different that she was the tiniest bit scared.

"That's good, Blazers!" Flora said approvingly. "What's that one called?"

Zaidee smiled wickedly. "Pure Evil."

"Awesome," Flora said. "I'm thinking you could hide in the dressing room next to my sister and do the ghost of Marie Antoinette."

Zaidee said, "The voice app is great. But we need something else to sell it."

They were silent for a second—prank planning was serious brain work. Then Zaidee spoke. "What if we got someone to use one of those fog machines to fill her dressing room with a smoky air? A kid at my old school had one and was always using it in the teachers' bathroom. I think we could order it really cheap online."

Flora was impressed. Blazers was better at being bad than she had expected.

"I like it!" Flora said. "But it can't be me. I need to be outside of the dressing room for deniability. And you'll be busy being the voice of Marie Antoinette."

Deniability was one of the words they always used on the cop show her father loved.

"What about Aidan and Aditya?"

"Those clowns?"

Zaidee didn't seem fazed. "I bet they'd be great at pranking."

Flora thought about it for a minute. "You're not wrong. I'll ask them."

CHAPTER 26

Ghosts Are Good, Frogs Are Not Okay

Aidan and Aditya had, unsurprisingly, said yes right away to the plan. The following weekend, it all went down. Maylin had gotten a call from the saleswoman saying to come in the next morning to see the new line of dresses.

Aidan and Aditya would get dropped off at the mall at ten a.m. After Maylin was situated in her dressing room, they would follow a random woman into the store and pretend to be with her.

Zaidee would arrive at the mall at 9:30 and hide out in the dressing room area. She'd then sneak into the room next to the quince-to-be as soon as Maylin arrived.

Maylin, Flora, and their mother would arrive a little after ten. Maylin would undoubtedly ask to see the new season of dresses in the brattiest of manners and stomp off to the dressing room like the Wicked Quincezilla of Eastern Rhode Island. Then the haunting would begin.

It was all going to plan. It helped that it was a stormy day, which Flora thought would only add to the ghostliness of it all. Flora could see Zaidee lurking discreetly in the dressing room. She spotted Aidan and Aditya standing outside the sporting goods shop across from the dress shop.

As soon as Maylin was settled in the dressing room, Zaidee signaled Aidan and Aditya.

Zaidee then entered the dressing room to the left of Maylin. Aidan and Aditya entered the dressing room to the right.

Luckily, Flora's mother had stepped outside of the store to take a call. She didn't know Zaidee, but she would have recognized the boys.

It turned out Aidan had a pocket-sized fog machine, so they were good to go on that front. He would pump fog into Maylin's dressing room and as soon as it was nice and thick, Zaidee would call out to Maylin in the voice of the ghost of Marie Antoinette.

The plan was *perfect*.

The boys filled the dressing room with fog, and Zaidee tapped her phone. A spooky voice called out in a creaky French accent: "Pretty dress, dear. You should absolutely buy that one."

But Maylin had been so busy staring into her own eyes and twirling in her dress that she didn't seem to notice.

Then the whole store went dark.

Flora could hear her mother call out, "Girls, are you okay?"

Maylin opened her dressing room door and said she was, although now she sounded unsure.

Flora said, "I'm okay too." She felt *muy valiente*, if she said so herself.

When the lights came back on, Aidan and Aditya were peering over the dressing room partition. Then, without warning, they dropped a giant, slimy red-eyed frog onto Maylin's head.

As Flora watched the frog's descent she thought, *Oh man, Maylin's going to howl like she's being murdered.*

But Maylin did not scream. She did not make a peep. She fainted. Passed out cold, right on the floor.

Flora, Zaidee, Aidan, and Aditya rushed to Maylin's dressing room and stood there, unsure of what to do. They weren't just busted. They could, Flora thought, potentially go to jail for this. What did they call it on that cop show? That's right: assault with intent to do bodily harm.

It was a very good thing that Flora's mother was a doctor. She figured out pretty quickly that although Maylin lay on the floor for what seemed like forever, she was actually in shock and not really hurt. Her mother reached into her purse and opened a jar of medical-grade smelling salts and waved it under Maylin's nose. Flora thought it smelled like the strongest toilet bowl cleaner.

The first thing that Maylin said when she came to was, "You, Flora, you planned this! I recognize your friends."

Flora's mother looked mad. She addressed Flora and her friends as if she were their mother. "Kids! What were you thinking?"

Aidan shrugged. "Fog made us think about frogs."

Aditya added, "And *frogs* seemed like an even better idea than *fog*."

Flora's mother shook her head. "Aidan, Aditya, how are you going to get home?"

"Our dad is downstairs in the book shop," Aidan said, staring guiltily at his shoes.

"Okay, I think you boys should go," Flora's mother said. She knew the twins well and for sure would be reporting their behavior to their mother.

Aidan and Aditya said, "Sorry, Maylin." Then they whispered, "Sorry, Flora" right before they walked away.

Maylin was sitting up, her back propped up against the dressing room door, fanning herself like a dama in distress.

"Are you okay?" Flora asked, meaning it.

"I think so," Maylin said dramatically.

"Flora, we don't know your other friend," her mother said, glancing over at Zaidee. "Do you two go to school together?

Zaidee sat on a chair in the dressing room across from Maylin and their mom.

"Yeah, she looks super grown-up, but this is Blaze—I mean, Zaidee," Flora said. "I went to her house to do homework a few weeks ago."

Flora's mother offered to drive Zaidee home. The girls got into the car and buckled their seat belts, and Flora requested that her mother play a soundtrack she'd made. But her mother said no.

Maylin sat in the front seat, staring straight ahead. "I could have had a heart attack. And died."

Flora's mother looked over at her and said, "I don't think so, querida."

Zaidee gave Flora a look, and Flora knew just what it meant: "We're in a heap of trouble, but we totally did something awesome."

Maylin, who was clearly feeling much better, since she was reapplying lip gloss in the car mirror, said, "I could have hit my head. Had a concussion and died."

This time, her mother didn't respond. Instead she turned to Flora and said, "Come on, girls, what were you thinking?"

Flora had to hide her smile. "We were just going to haunt Maylin with the ghost of Marie Antoinette."

Zaidee added, "Because Marie Antoinette was obsessed with fashion."

Flora could see her mother's expression in the

rearview mirror. She looked more confused than mad. "But what do frogs have to do with Marie Antoinette?"

Flora shrugged. "We have no idea. That was Aidan and Aditya's idea. We were as surprised as you were!"

"Quelle folie!" Zaidee said.

"Using animals like that, not okay," Flora said sternly, hopeful that showing remorse would lessen the punishment that was certainly coming her way.

"Hmmm," her mother said. Then she turned on Flora's Broadway playlist and didn't speak for the rest of the ride.

CHAPTER 27

Grounded

When they got home, Flora's mother called a doctor at the hospital who assured her that Maylin did not likely have a concussion, but that she should stay awake and be observed closely.

Maylin was situated on the couch with a tray of snacks and the remote. Normally Flora would angle for room on the couch and control of the TV, but she felt bad that Maylin had been scared by their prank.

"Why would you even do that?" Maylin asked, her eyes wet with what Flora was sure was fake tears. "What did I ever do to you?"

Flora snorted. She wanted to say, "Give me a month and I'll make you a list."

Then it occurred to her: Maybe Maylin's main goal in life wasn't making her miserable. Or maybe it was just the power of the both/and. Maybe Maylin could be *both* a monster *and* a scaredy cat at the same time.

Their parents came into the living room. Her father looked more disappointed than angry, which was always worse, somehow.

"Flora, you're grounded for a month," he said. "No after-school hangouts with this girl Zaidee. We're concerned that she's a bad influence."

"Are you kidding me?" Flora said. "Blazers is as goody two-shoes as they come. The prank was my idea."

"So *you're* the bad influence?" her father said.

Flora nodded. It was important to her that her parents didn't think badly of her new friend.

"Can I still go to dance class on Wednesday nights?" Flora asked. "I love that class.

Her father said, "That's really up to Maylin."

Maylin looked up and said, "I don't know . . ."

Flora liked the dance class so much, she was not above begging. "Please, Maylin."

"Fine," Maylin said, rolling her eyes.

"Thank you so much," Flora said. "I promise you

won't regret it. And I promise: From now on, I'm going to be the best quince helper you've ever seen. Your wish is my command."

Maylin smirked, the right corner of her mouth turning up ever so slightly. "Well, I like the sound of that."

The next day at breakfast, Flora cracked open her notebook. "Sometimes I forget things, so I'm going to write down everything you need me to do."

Her mother looked impressed. "Tan responsable."

Maylin was blending her morning smoothie. "Okay, niña. This is a big one. Make sure to write it down."

Flora uncapped her favorite blue pen. "Ready."

"Nobody likes a kiss-up," Maylin said.

Their father looked disapprovingly at Maylin. "Maylin. Your sister is trying to help."

"Fine." Maylin rolled her eyes. "I need to get thank-you notes. I wanted to get monogrammed stationery, but I haven't seen any that I like."

"I can make them for you."

Maylin looked doubtful. "A mí me gustaría algo más elegante."

Flora said, "I can do elegant! Papá, if you could take me to the art supply store after school, I could get supplies and show you different styles."

"Okay, but don't get your hopes up," Maylin said. "I have serious doubts that you could do something as professional as I need."

Flora grinned. She was beginning to like being underestimated. It reminded her of a sign she loved in Bruce Lee Boba, a quote from Bruce Lee that said: "If I tell you I'm good, probably you will say I'm boasting. But if I tell you I'm not good, you'll know I'm lying."

She decided she wouldn't tell Maylin anything. She would just show her.

The next day after school, Zaidee called out to her just as she was approaching the playground.

"Hey Flora, are you still on punishment?"

"Yeah."

"Are you headed to your dad's shop?"

Flora said she was.

"I'll walk you," Zaidee said, and Flora smiled. It was such a Clara thing to do.

As they walked through Wilcox Park, Zaidee said, "I'm sorry our first prank was such a disaster."

"It's okay, Blazers."

Zaidee said, "I got the invite to Maylin's quince. I'm surprised she even invited me after the frog debacle."

Flora grinned. "My mom made her so I could have someone to hang out with."

"Well, I can't wait. I've never been to a quince."

At the shop, the girls waved goodbye and Flora made her way to the desk in the back that she had claimed as her own.

Flora raced through her homework assignments. Math—easy. English—medium hard. She took out her sketch pad and began free-drawing designs she'd researched online.

The first example was a traditional script. A big *M* in the middle and then an *A* and an *L* on either side for Maylin's middle and last name, Abril and LeFevre.

Using the Photoshop program that Clara's mom had given her, Flora drew the letters in magenta and orange, as well as a more traditional silver and black.

The second design had Maylin's first name in cursive and her last name in block print. Flora liked this a lot. Then she added the address on the bottom.

It was okay. Better than she thought she would've been able to do. But it wasn't Bruce Lee boast-worthy. Flora decided to keep working at it.

A week later, an impatient Maylin wanted to see the designs.

"How are those thank-you cards going?" Maylin asked over breakfast. "You know the quince is less than a month away."

"I just want them to be perfect."

That afternoon, Flora had an idea. She emailed the designs to Clara's mom and she gave her tips on the color of the ink and placement of the text.

The third design was the toughest. Flora thought that Maylin's quince thank-you notes should actually have a picture of Maylin on them. She kept doubting herself. Nothing she drew in her sketchbook felt good enough.

Then one day after school, she got a text from Clara's mom:

"Flora, cuando tengas un momentito, llámame. I have an idea."

Tía Mariana said, "Do you have Maylin's quince portrait?"

Flora did.

"You can use that in Photoshop to make a black-and-white pencil sketch that you can use to make a watercolor portrait."

"But isn't that cheating?" Flora asked.

"No way," Tía Mariana said. "It's using technology. Even Michelangelo used mirrors to make his art."

That night, over Zoom, Tía Mariana coached Flora on how to make the sketch. Flora's dad sat next to her, ready to help.

Flora paused as the image filled the screen. It was a beautiful photo of Maylin holding a quince bouquet of blue and purple hydrangeas. She had to give it to her sister. She looked so pretty—and grown-up.

"First," Tía Mariana said. "We have to take all the

color out of the image. You do that by turning the saturation all the way down, to negative one hundred."

Flora did as she was advised and the picture of Maylin went to black and white.

"Bueno, Flora!" Clara's mom said. "Now you're going to invert the picture."

All of a sudden Maylin's face looked like the negative of a film, a black border filled with gray.

"Then you apply a blur filter," Tía Mariana said. "See, you're doing the work. Technology is a great tool for artists."

Flora looked at the screen; it was a black-and-white outline of Maylin's portrait that looked like it had been drawn in pencil. It looked just like her.

"That's pretty cool," her dad said. "Gracias, Mariana."

Mariana smiled across the tablet screen. "Ah, it's nothing. Flora did all the work. Now you can print as many copies as you like onto watercolor paper. Use that as the basis for your sketch."

"I'm so excited," Flora said.

"Me too. It's very kind of you to work so hard on this gift for your sister. Okay, I better go. But email me and let me know how it's going."

"We miss you so much," Flora said quietly, thinking of how long it had been since she could just walk down the street to Clara's house.

"Oh, we miss you too. Clara's trying to make new friends, but no one will ever replace you, Flora. You're more than a friend; you're the sister Clara never had."

Mariana blew a kiss to the screen. And then she was gone.

CHAPTER 28

Watercolors

For the next three days, each day after school, Flora did watercolor paintings of Maylin at her father's shop. He laid newspaper out on the desk and she set up her brushes and paints.

She made tiny tweaks to Maylin's skin, trying to get the exact right shade of honey brown. Maylin's hair was easy—her cascading wavy hair was made for watercolors. Flora added flecks of golden brown to the jet-black hair, to give her sister the highlights she was always begging for.

Next, she played with the lavender color of Maylin's dress and the rhinestone accents of the crown. The best part was painting Maylin's bouquet. Flora thought she could play forever with the deepest blues and purples of the cloud-like petals and the bright green leaves of the bouquet.

Finally, when she had a version she was happy with, she added a pinkish red blush to Maylin's cheek and silver lavender tinge to the rhinestones in her quince crown.

She cut the card into a large square. Then on the back of the card, using a calligraphy pen, she wrote at the top of the card:

Mil Gracias. Su amiga, Maylin.

"Papá," she said softly. "I think I'm done."

Her father walked over to the desk and his eyes widened as he took her artwork in.

"Flora, querida," he said. "That is beyond beautiful."

He grabbed her in an embrace. "I could not be more proud of you. The talent and the time you poured into this was extraordinary."

Flora liked hearing that he was proud of her.

"Do you think Maylin will like it?"

"Like? She'll love it."

When it came time to close the shop for the day, her father helped her carefully place the final image into a folder and then into the leather portfolio her father used for his most important designs.

When they got home, her mother was standing at the stove, cooking. The kitchen was flooded with the sounds of salsa music.

Maylin sat at the kitchen island, studying a makeup tutorial on how to do the perfect cat-eye like it was a Khan Academy video on quantum physics.

Flora sat next to her.

Her father washed his hands, then held her mother by the waist, pulling her toward him. Her parents started dancing together. Flora smiled—they were so good. She bet they could've been professional salseros.

Maylin was unamused. "Come on! Are you dancing or cooking?"

Flora, who loved watching her parents dance, said, "No seas tan estúpida. They are doing both."

Of course, it was the "estúpida" comment that got her mother's attention. "Flora," her mother admonished her. "Speak respectfully, mija!"

"But she's the one being rude," Flora whinged.

She couldn't believe that she had spent her every free moment working on Maylin's quince thank-you notes. She was so mad that she had a mind just to rip all the samples up.

After dinner that night, as he served them each a scoop of mango chili sorbet, Flora's father asked, "Do you have something to show Maylin, Flora?"

Flora tried to give him her best Darth Vader glare.

"No sé, Papá," she said.

"I think you do," he said, heading to the table in the entryway of the house and returning with the leather portfolio. "Here you go."

"Thanks, Papá," Flora said grumpily. When she got older she was going to change her middle name to "Okay, you win," because that was her life story. She was Flora "Okay, you win" LeFevre and she'd always be second place to Maylin, no matter how badly her sister behaved.

Finding an ice cream–free place on the dining table, Flora said, "Maylin, I have three options to show you."

"It's about time," Maylin said.

"The first is a traditional monogram."

Maylin looked it over. "Wow, I'm impressed. I could definitely use this one."

"Option two is a little more playful."

Flora showed her sister the card with her first name in script and her last name in block type.

"This is definitely the one. It's classy but cool. Well done."

Their mother said, "Could I place an order for my own notecards in style two. A mí me cae bien."

"Sure!" Flora said. "Tía Mariana gave me the name of a print shop in New Haven that can make copies on cardstock in forty-eight hours."

"But there's one more," her father said, winking at Flora.

Maylin said, "No necesito verlo. I like number two, and I pride myself on being very decisive."

"I think you'll want to see this," their dad said.

Flora held the folder with the watercolor in her hand. To her surprise, her hand was shaking a little. If Maylin didn't like it, if she said something mean, Flora knew that she was going to cry.

Her father seemed to read her mind. He put a

reassuring hand on her shoulder and gave it a squeeze. "It's okay, Flora. Show her."

Flora spoke softly. "I wanted to do one more style that really captured how amazing you will look in your quince portrait. I'm sorry we pulled that stupid prank when you were trying on dresses. I hope you have the best quince ever."

She could see her parents exchange glances.

Maylin looked surprised to hear Flora's apology. "Wow, gracias hermana," she said in a gentle voice.

Flora took out the watercolor portrait and laid it on the table. She took it in for a second. The drawing looked extra beautiful framed by the wood of her father's table.

She felt her mother's arms around her. "Ay niña, eres una maravilla. This is one of the most beautiful things I've ever seen."

Maylin was unusually quiet.

Then she said, "It looks just like me. How'd you *do* that?"

Flora shrugged. "I got a lot of help from Tía Mariana."

Her father said, "But you put in hours and hours

of work to get it just right. Show her the back of the card."

"Mil gracias. Su amiga, Maylin," her sister whispered, reading the text. "It's perfect. It's better than perfect."

She turned to Flora then and asked, "You did all of this for me?"

Flora nodded. "Of course. Hermanas take care of each other."

Then her sister did something she hadn't done since they were both in elementary school. Maylin held her close, and for what felt to Flora like a very long time, she did not let her go.

CHAPTER 29

A Quince Miracle

No one in Flora's house slept the night before the quince except for Maylin. Flora's mother and her tía Janet were making empanadas for the reception, using Tía Mariana's recipe. They could have purchased them, but even working double shifts all week at the hospital couldn't keep Flora's mother from making them herself.

Her father sat in the living room watching highlights of the Copa América game, while absentmindedly filling party bags with quince favors for all of the guests.

"Presta atención," her mother said, without even looking into the room. "I'm sure you're missing a few."

Flora's father winked at her as he looked down at the bags. "I'll fix them," he said. "And no one will be the wiser."

Flora smiled. "I'll help you, Papá."

She sat, legs crisscrossed on the floor, next to the table with the bags and had just started inspecting them to see which ones needed fixing when she heard a loud knock on the door.

Her mother called out, "Flora! Can you get the door?"

Flora wondered, *Who rings the doorbell at seven a.m.?* But she knew it could be anyone—the tent guy or the caterer or the florist. There were so many people involved in the coronation of Maylin that her father hung a giant bulletin board in the kitchen with pictures, cell phone numbers, and multi-colored Post-its. Green meant the person was good to go. Yellow meant someone needed calling back, and blue was for all the things that had been double-checked.

"Just looking at this board gives me a headache," Flora said, pausing to take it all in.

"Flora!" her mother yelled out once again. "¡La puerta!"

As she bolted toward the door, Flora called out, "I'm coming! I'm coming!"

As if whoever had the gall to ring the door at seven a.m. might leave if she didn't answer right away. (She loved the word *gall*. She had learned it from Zaidee, and what she loved the most was how bored and cool it made her sound.)

She didn't even bother to look through the peephole, as that would have involved dragging a chair to the door so she could get high enough to see. She just flung the door open.

"¡Hola!" Clara said.

Flora blinked. *Clara?*

"Flora, you should have asked who it was," Tía Mariana said, shaking her finger in that tía way. Clara and her mother were standing on her front porch as they had a gazillion times before. As if they had just walked three blocks instead of flown three thousand miles.

"Are you going to let us in?" Tía Mariana said.

"I think she's in shock," Clara said decisively. She mimed moving an invisible stethoscope to Flora's heart.

Flora shook her head in disbelief.

"No?" Clara asked, clearly enjoying the power of her surprise. "Do you want us to go?"

Then Flora pulled Clara in for a hug so tight that she feared she might pop Clara like a balloon.

Flora's mother came from the kitchen and said, "Flora! Invite them in! It's cold out there."

It was an early May morning—the Saturday of Memorial Day weekend. Even at seven a.m., Westerly was a mild sixty degrees. But to a Panamanian, Flora knew, that was pretty cold.

"I can't believe you're here," Flora whispered to Clara as she carried her and Tía Mariana's bags up to the guest room. "I think I'm dreaming."

Clara felt Flora's forehead. "You don't have a fever."

Then Clara squeezed her own cheeks, "And I'm one hundred percent really here. So it's not a dream!"

Breakfast was a rowdy Panamanian-style affair. Tío Rogelio and Tío Luca were there with Delfina, who had just started to walk. Maylin sat at the head of the table and to her right was her best friend, Frankie, who had spent the night. Flora's tía Janet was there as well as Flora's parents and, of course, Clara and Tía Mariana.

"You're actually really and truly here," Flora said, taking absentminded bites of her hojalda.

"I am."

Tía Mariana said, "When I saw how hard you were working on Maylin's quince, I booked the tickets for us the very next day, Flora. We wanted to be here for the event, but I also realized that you and Clara were in need of an amiga fix."

"I missed you," Flora said.

"Me too," Clara said.

"But you like California . . ."

"It's different," Clara explained. "You'll see when you come visit."

Flora flopped her elbow on the table, knowing her parents were too busy to notice.

"How long will you stay?"

"Till Tuesday."

Three whole nights, Flora thought. It seemed like a lifetime and no time at all.

CHAPTER 30

Sister Act

It was sunset when the family arrived back at the house for Maylin's quince celebration. The whole family, along with Clara and Tía Mariana, had gone to the church for service, then to the beach for pictures. While they were away, their backyard had been transformed. A giant tent went all the way from the house down to the little creek in their backyard. Tables surrounded the periphery. In the center of the tent, there was a dance floor with a light that shined a giant cursive *M* onto the middle of the floor. Fairy lights hung across the top of the tent, casting twinkly shadows across the dance floor.

Zaidee walked into the tent and Flora gave her a hug. "I'm glad you're here!"

"Me too!"

Zaidee looked up and gasped. "It looks like a million . . ."

"Stars," Flora whispered.

Flora felt nervous introducing Clara to Zaidee. She didn't want Clara to think she'd replaced her. But when Zaidee arrived at the quince, she knew it was like a Band-Aid: She just had to do it quickly.

Speaking faster than her mother flinging Spanish at someone who made her mad, Flora said, "Clara-I-want-you-to-meet-my-new-friend-Zaidee."

"Hola, Zaidee."

"Nice to meet you."

Clara peered closely at Zaidee. She asked, "Anyone ever tell you that you look like a high school kid?"

Zaidee smiled. "I get that a lot. My parents are tall."

"So what's our plan of attack?" Clara asked, linking arms with Flora and Zaidee.

"Are we attacking someone?" Zaidee asked, looking confused.

"Not someone, something: food," Clara explained.

"All of that delicious food. That's the best part of quinceañeras: the grub."

"Empanadas," Flora said decisively. "Then cake. Then the hot chocolate bar."

And suddenly, it felt good to have both Clara and Zaidee there. It felt like the sun and the moon were shining at the very same time.

Maylin danced a classical waltz with their father. Then their father and mother danced together. Flora was supposed to come out next and dance with her cousin Francisco, who was twelve. But Francisco was more than happy to sit the dance out and play video games in the living room. Luckily, the next set of the quince court glided onto the dance floor before she could even notice.

Flora went to say hello to her abuela and found her chismeando in Spanish with a group of older women. Mr. Carter, Abuela's gentleman friend, was sitting at a table by himself, so Flora went over to say hi.

She said, "Hey, Mr. Carter. Do you mind when Abuela is speaking Spanish and you don't understand?"

He smiled and said, "Every day, your grandmother tells me, 'Te amo, Julius.' That's all the Spanish I need to know."

Flora smiled.

"You know, Flora," Mr. Carter said. "One of these days, all of this fanfare is going to be for you. Your grandmother and I look forward to dancing at your quinceañera."

Flora liked the way he said the Spanish word, slowly and carefully, as if each syllable was dripped in honey.

"Oh, I'm not going to have a fancy quince, Mr. Carter," she said. "All this isn't for me."

Abuela returned and put her arms around Mr. Carter. "Do you hear that, Julius? It's Ella and Louis. I think that's our cue to dance."

Mr. Carter rose and took Abuela's hand. "Yes, ma'am."

Then he turned to Flora. "Don't be so sure that you're not the big ball gown quince type, Flora. I, for one, think you'd be smashing at a party like this."

Flora watched him twirl her abuela onto the dance floor.

She found Clara and Zaidee sitting in the yard in front of Tío Rogelio's house, right in front of the wooden dance floor that a crew had installed at six o'clock that morning.

Maylin lined up with her court, half whispering, half yelling instructions, "Remember. It's a cross formation. We start with the waltz, then when the DJ drops the beat, we hit the merengue, into the cumbia, and then the bhangra body roll."

The music started and the court took center stage. Seven girls. Seven boys. And Maylin in the middle as number fifteen.

The music started slow and the boys, especially, seemed uncomfortable with the more formal dance moves.

Maylin kept counting, loud enough that the other guests could hear. "It's a one and a two, three and a four, snap, cross, turn, then jump."

Maylin stopped dancing and looked around frustrated. "Why is no one jumping?!"

The dancers in Maylin's court tried to keep up with her instructions, but some of them, inevitably, started moving to their own beat.

Maylin signaled the DJ. "Stop the music! Stop the music!"

Then she looked at her dancers, her eyes thick.

Clara said, "I can see that Maylin the Monster is up to her old tricks."

Flora sighed, "Ay. It looks like Maylin is in retrograde. Let me go talk to her."

Clara said, "Do we not hate her anymore? You gotta catch me up on who we're hating."

Flora shrugged. "We hate her a little less."

She walked over to Maylin, whose two best friends were trying to comfort her.

"Come on, Maylin, the party is hot," Frankie said reassuringly.

Jade chimed in, "Westerly's never seen anything like this, chica. Trust."

Nina, the choreographer, tried to help. She said, "Hey Maylin, calm down. It's all good as long as everyone is having fun."

"Why should I calm down?" Maylin said. "We have been practicing for months and we look like the sizzle reel for *America's Got No Talent*."

"It doesn't matter, Maylin. Just shake it off. All that matters is that you're having fun."

"It's not 'fun' for me that my showcase dance that's supposed to be lit is so raggedy."

Flora felt bad that Maylin was so upset, but even more, she didn't want their family and friends to remember Maylin's quince as a scene from one of those *My Super Sweet 16* meltdowns. She looked over at her sister and saw just how afraid her sister was of being embarrassed. "Maylin, I know you notice everything they are doing wrong," Flora said softly. "But the guests don't know. It just looks like some people are freestyling their solos."

Maylin growled. "Pero, esto no sirve. It's my quince. Nobody solos but me."

Nina put her arm around Maylin. "Really Maylin, it doesn't matter how it all starts. What matters is how you end it. Let's regroup and figure out how to finish it strong. I think the next dance should just be you and your sister. She knows all the moves."

Maylin laughed. A mean, wicked witch laugh that made Flora feel bad. She said, "She's ten. I'm not having my big quince moment with my bratty little sister."

Nina was insistent. "You should dance with her, Maylin. She's really good."

Maylin considered for a moment. Flora tried to stop hopping up and down with excitement, but she couldn't.

Flora said, "Maylin, I promise. I know all of the steps. I'll make you look good."

Maylin was quiet for what felt like a very long time.

"Okay," she said. "But Flora, ya verás, if you ruin this for me, I will find five million ways to end your life."

Flora smiled. She was starting to realize that the more nervous Maylin got, the more ridiculous her threats became.

"Come on, hermana," Flora said. "We got this."

Maylin and Flora walked out onto the dance floor and at their cue, the DJ flipped the music from a classic Spanish ballad to a bumping reggaeton.

The two girls ran out onto the dance floor and together, they rolled their shoulders, swerved and curved, stomped and grooved. Nina had given Flora the best advice—she said, "Don't think about the steps, just listen, really listen to the music, and you'll be fine."

At first, when the steps all seemed mysterious and impossible, Flora didn't believe her. But the more they moved, the more Flora could feel it.

Nina told Flora that the choreography was less about the fancy footwork but really about finding the two or three moves that you could do with confidence. "And smile," Nina said. "Everybody looks better when they're having fun."

Nina also shared what she considered to be the best trick she ever learned in a dance class. "If you forget a move, just turn to the crowd and do the universal 'louder louder' move with your hand. It's like you're inviting them to get involved. I call it 'the rapper.'"

It was helpful to feel like there was a "get out of the choreography" card if everything went wrong. But everything went right. Flora didn't forget a single move.

She looked around and could see Clara and Zaidee were standing and swaying back and forth. Her parents looked so happy. It almost seemed like a dream. At the very end, Flora grabbed Maylin's hand, Maylin spun out, and then they popped and locked toward each other, ending with a champeta routine that got them a standing ovation from the entire room. When they were done, there was wild applause. Flora looked in the crowd for her family. Flora's parents, her uncles, and her grandmother were clapping their hands and smiling broadly.

The DJ ran another reggaeton classic and Flora and Maylin ran around pulling their friends and family onto the dance floor. Flora's parents joined them, her father showing off his signature early 2000s moves. Her abuela merengued onto the floor. Maylin's friends joined in, as did Clara and Zaidee. Flora couldn't believe how much fun it was.

When they all sat down, her tío Rogelio went up to the DJ booth and took the microphone. He said, "Give it up for my sobrinas! Flora and Maylin!"

The hundred or so people that filled the yard

between Flora's house and her uncles' clapped and stomped their feet. Flora loved that Panamanians never did one thing—just clapping—when two things—clapping and stomping—would do.

Tío Rogelio asked everyone to raise their glass in a toast to the quince girl and he said, "We're here to celebrate our quinceañera, Maylin Abril Candela Castillo LeFevre. In our culture, fifteen is the beginning of a new chapter in a young woman's life. Maylin, we can hardly wait to see what you do with your life and all of your gifts. But we want you to know that we are all here—not just for the empanadas and the dulce de leche, but to let you and your parents know that nosotros te tenemos. We'll be here to support you and lift you up every step of the way."

When all the speeches were done, the girls made their way to the hot chocolate bar and filled their tin mugs with hot gooey chocolate and all the fixings.

"That was ah-mazing," Clara sighed.

"It was fun. But you know, I don't think all of this

quince princess stuff is for me," Flora said, surveying the scene.

"Me neither," Clara agreed.

"You might change your mind in five years when you're turning fifteen," Zaidee said.

"I guess you're right," Flora said.

"Nah, never going to happen," Clara said.

"My mom said that if I didn't want to have a quince, they could use the money they would've spent on a big party to take me and a friend on a trip," Flora explained.

"Oooh," Clara said, rubbing her hands together, as if plotting. "Where would you go?"

"I dunno," Flora said. "Maybe Paris."

"Not very Panamanian of you, Flora," Clara said.

"I know," Flora said. "But I want to hunt down the ghost of Marie Antoinette."

Zaidee laughed and said, "Do you think your parents might let you invite two friends?"

Flora sniffed. "I sure hope so. I mean look at this shindig. DJ. Tents. Dance floor. Caterers. Florists. This party cuesta una fortuna."

"I could come along as your translator," Zaidee said.

"That's the stuff," Clara said. "Can you translate that for me?"

"C'est le truc," Zaidee said.

"I like it," Clara said, extending her hand for Zaidee to shake. "You're hired."

Flora didn't say anything. She sat quietly taking in the fairy lights, all of their family and friends laughing and dancing under the stars. Zaidee had turned out to be a real friend. Clara hadn't forgotten about her. Somehow, the Humpty Dumpty pieces of her life had come back together again. Clara had been right. It was a quince miracle.

In comic books when characters from different universes come together, like in the Spider-Verse, everything goes wrong. The saying was: Worlds collide.

But Flora seemed to have pulled it off. Worlds had collided but it was all good. She had a new friend and her forever friend and even things with her big sister were going better than expected. She took a deep breath and marveled at how sweet the salt air was.

Clara looked over at her. "Flora, are you smelling the sea?"

She nodded. She was, and just like her uncle said, it smelled like home.

ACKNOWLEDGMENTS

This book is inspired by my daughter Flora and her friend Clara. Their friendship started when we all lived in Palo Alto and the girls were nine. Then we moved back home to New York and now we live in London, but Flora and Clara's friendship is still going strong. There are always tears when they part but so much laughter whenever they get together.

When I was Flora's age, I was very invested in having one best friend who scored off the charts in the B-F-F-ometer. But as I got older, I had the good luck to meet an array of friends—each with their own kind of magic and each game to join me in all kinds of adventures. Some of my favorite friends now are people who I thought would never like me because they were so cool, so beautiful, so smart and well-put together. I've learned that nobody ever really sees themselves the way you think they do and that friendship can grow where you least expect it.

So for all the lessons about the art of friendship, I want to thank a few of my most beloved amigas like Steffi Michel and Clara's mom, Mariana, who met me mid-meltdown and swept in to save the day, as well as newer amigas like Erica Green and Megumi Ikeda. This book was also bolstered by steady sista fixes with my querida Caroline Kim Oh.

Gracias y abrazos to my editor Nancy Mercado, who sees me and helps me bring the stories I came to tell to the page. I'm grateful for the able, thoughtful hands of associate editor Rosie Ahmed and the copyediting of Regina Castillo and Margarita Javier. It's so much fun to work with the whole Dial team, including the amazing Elyse Marshall and the ace visuals team: designer Cerise Steel and art director Jennifer Kelly.

Quince crowns and freshly made empanadas to Kimberly Witherspoon, Jessica Mileo, and the whole Inkwell Management team. Jason Clampet is my concolon, the goodness at the end of every long day.

I had the great fortune to be part of the inaugural class of makers who got to attend a retreat at Milkwood, a truly one of a kind retreat for the children's book community. For all the inspiration, good food, and encouragement, thank you to Sophie Blackall and Ed Schmidt.

Finally, thank you to my dear friend Sujean Rim for bringing Flora and her world to life with her beautiful illustrations. Sujean, I just feel lucky to know you—on and off the page.